ENDLESS LOVE

ELITE HEIRS OF MANHATTAN BOOK 6

MISSY WALKER

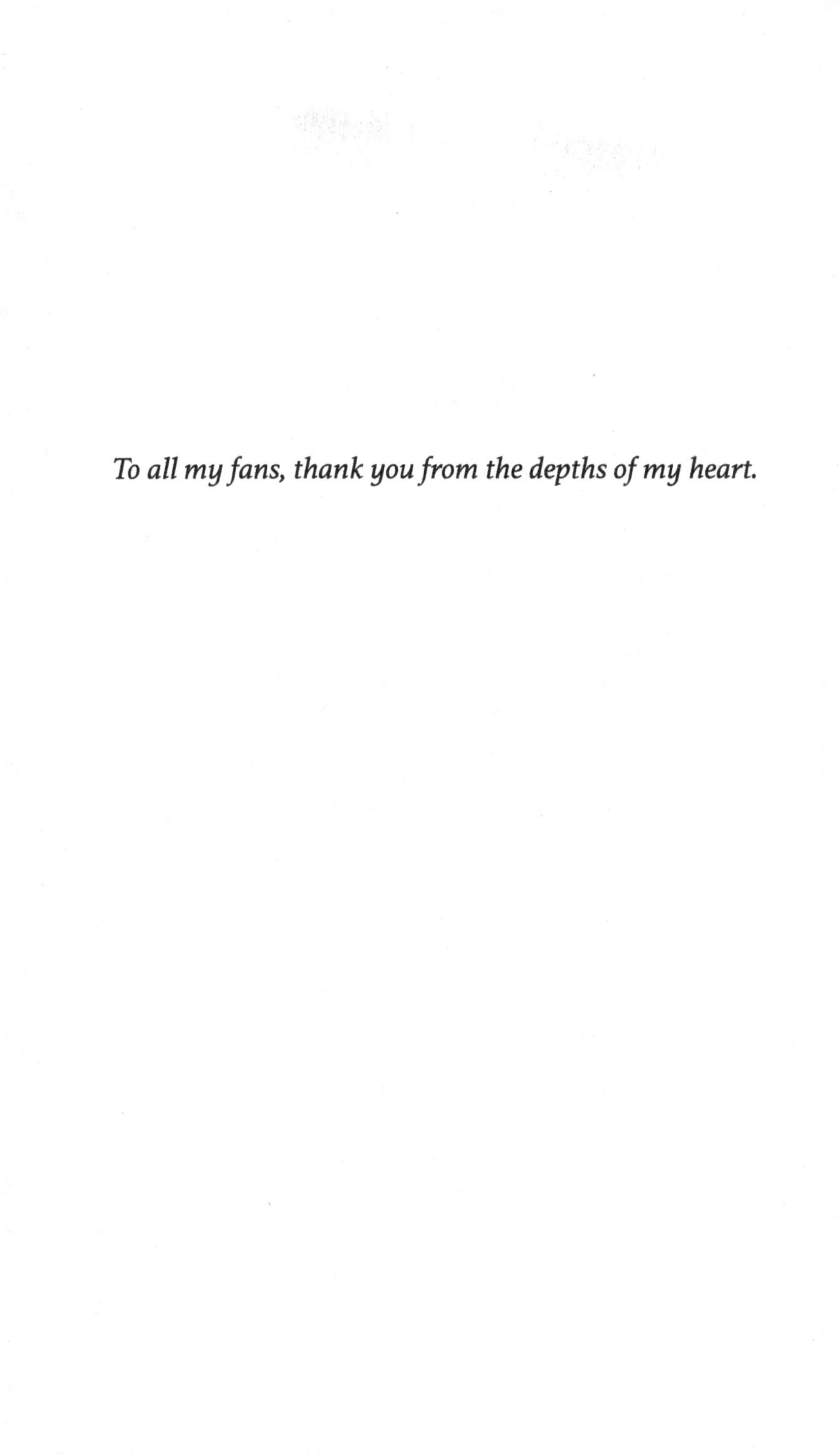

To all my fans, thank you from the depths of my heart.

Elite *Men* Of Manhattan and
Elite *Heirs* of Manhattan Family Tree

1

____

COLTON

"We'd better get moving." It was the third time I'd tried to remind my wife of a schedule we needed to keep this weekend. "I don't feel like getting my eyes clawed out by Valentina," I added.

"I'm sure it's bad luck for a bride to claw out the eyes of one of the groomsmen," Rose pointed out with a gentle laugh as she finished hanging up the last of the bridesmaids' dresses, then stepped back with a satisfied smile.

As always, seeing her like that filled my heart until breathing was tough. Before her, I didn't know what it meant to watch the woman I loved take so much pleasure and purpose from her work.

This wasn't about work, though. She would wear

one of those dresses in three days, as would my sister, Sienna. The other two gowns were concealed by opaque garment bags, being stored in Rose's office until the night before the ceremony.

When I cast an interested look in that direction, Rose swatted me away. "You're not allowed to look, remember?"

"I'm not the groom," I reminded her. "Don't worry. If either Miles or Evan wander in here to get a glimpse, I'll keep them away. Whatever it takes." I gave a sarcastic salute, and my wife rolled her eyes.

"I'm just saying..." running a hand through her soft, blonde hair, she sighed, "... this would be stressful enough for everybody if it were just one wedding, but a double wedding? That's double the chance for something to go wrong."

"I don't remember you being this nervous for our wedding." I slid my arms around her waist and touched my nose to the top of her head. The floral fragrance of her shampoo made me smile. The scent of lilacs always left me thinking of her.

"That was different," she insisted, snuggling into me. "Our wedding was just... the next natural thing to do. But this? The happiness of our friends and family hangs on this. Everything has to be perfect."

"And it will be. It already is," I reminded her,

tightening my grip when she relaxed against me. "Everything is going perfectly. Even for a double wedding, it's going off without a hitch."

That didn't mean there hadn't been a fair share of drama. Valentina and Evan got engaged the day their daughter was born a little more than a year ago. They'd focused on building their life together, which meant raising their daughter and growing their businesses. It didn't seem to matter to either of them when they were married.

It took Aria and Miles' engagement six months later to light a fire under their asses. Aria had wanted to roll straight into wedding planning rather than wait, then soon, there were whispers of a double wedding. I shrugged it off as a joke for a while, but it was obvious the girls were serious.

Since then, there had been countless conversations, plans were made and then discarded, but finally, it was decided the twins would be married at my family's Hamptons estate, with Mom and Aunt Evelyn in charge of the finer details. "*I will not have you stressing out over planning your own wedding,*" Aunt Evelyn had told Valentina during a family get-together when the wedding planning was first underway. "*You are going to sit back, relax as much as a bride can, and let somebody else handle the details for once. All you have to do is tell us what you want."*

Right, like getting two strong personalities to agree on anything would be easy. Somehow, they'd made it work, and now we were three short days away from what the media was referring to as the wedding of the decade. The daughters of Magnus Miller, entrepreneur and philanthropist, are getting hitched in grand style. It was the sort of event people salivated over that would give engaged girls and those looking for a ring plenty to inspire them.

Meaning Rose's end had to be perfect to reflect the family brand. "Farrah Goldsmith couture will come out looking like the obvious choice for any discerning bride," I predicted, kissing the top of my wife's head. "Let's get out of here. I'm sure Mom has been pulling her hair out, handling last-minute stuff while keeping an eye on Eloise."

Just the mention of my daughter brought a smile to my face, even in the context of her being a holy terror when she felt like it. At eighteen months, she was a speed demon with the power to disappear at will and wind up exactly where she wasn't supposed to be.

"I'll only need a few seconds," Rose assured me, flipping the lights off around the store and double-checking the lock on the door once we were outside. It was a clear, beautiful night, perfect for a clambake on the beach.

"Now, your only job this weekend is to have fun," I reminded her after opening the passenger door of my Mustang. "Understood?"

"Ooh. Is that an order?" she asked with a flirtatious grin when sliding into the car and crossing one lean leg over the other. The hem of her pencil skirt crept up her thigh as she purred, "You know what it does to me when you get all growly and insistent."

I leaned down, murmuring, "Tell me more. What does it do to you?" Because even though we were on our way to spend the evening with family, I couldn't resist flirting with my wife.

"I'll show you later." She quickly kissed me, pulled the door closed, and left me laughing as I rounded the car.

There was no laughing when I took hold of her knee as I slipped behind the wheel, letting my fingers creep under her skirt's hem. Two years of marriage, and it still took nothing to excite me. Already my thoughts were buzzing with the possibility of sneaking off with her sometime tonight. As nice as it would be to get together with the family ahead of everybody else descending on East Hampton, I would much rather have spent the night devouring every inch of the woman sitting beside me.

"You better behave yourself," she teased, swatting my hand away. "Remember. We have to play nice in front of the grownups."

The idea left me snickering as I pulled away from the store. "Please. You've seen the looks my parents still give each other when they think nobody's watching."

"Mine, too," she pointed out, chuckling. "It's nice, though. That will be us one day."

She had a way of saying simple things like that and cracking my heart open to make more room. "You're right," I told her, took her hand again, and lifted it to my lips. There was no chance of life going any other way. I couldn't imagine a time when I wouldn't need her the way I needed air.

There was nothing like making the turn onto the grounds of the family estate when it was full of light and life. The sprawling house gleamed like a jewel, all the lights on the first floor burning bright against the dusk that had begun to fall.

In three days, it would be transformed into something even more impressive than ever. There would be tents set up on the grounds and on the beach, lit by twinkling lights and torches before the reception, and the equivalent of an entire conservatory's worth of flowers would be set up everywhere possible.

"We want to make this memorable," Mom had insisted more than once. *"All eyes will be on the family."* I couldn't remember her being this anxious before my wedding, but then there was something extra special and attention worthy since two brides were now involved. I might have called it a gimmick in my more cynical days, but now I knew better. Rose had softened me in the best way.

A dozen cars were already parked in the circular courtyard. "Looks like we're just about the last ones to get here," Rose observed, craning her neck as she looked around. "I see Evan and Valentina's cars. The Spectre belongs to Lucian, doesn't it? So he and Ivy are probably here already."

"There's still plenty of time before dinner. We haven't held anybody up." Over the years, I had come to understand the ways we balanced each other out. Whenever she got a little too high-strung, too up in her head, I knew how to bring her back down to reality.

"I know, you're right." She laughed at herself and

waved a hand, then unbuckled her belt. "Come on. I'm sure Eloise misses us."

As usual, the mention of my daughter brought a smile to my face. She had me wrapped around her finger.

I had a spring in my step when I exited the car and took Rose's hand, the two of us climbing the steps to the deep porch. The dull roar I could hear standing outside became something almost deafening when I opened the door. A wall of voices slammed into us, led by one of the brides. "I'm just saying, I think it makes more sense for us to go down the aisle separately." We rounded the entry hall, heading into the main room where Valentina gestured with the wine glass she held. "So we could both have a chance to shine."

A trio of sofas were arranged in a U-shape, and across them were our friends and family. Aria sat with her legs stretched out across Miles' lap, and it looked like he was deliberately holding her in place when she blurted out, "For the hundredth time, that makes no goddamn sense!"

"We can still leave before anybody notices us," I whispered to my wife, who gave my arm a playful slap as we ventured deeper into the house.

"She has a point." Evan, of course, took his

fiancée's side. "This way, you could both get your moment on your dad's arm." My sister, Sienna, sat on the other end of the sofa he was perched on, and she shot me a pleading look when I caught her eye. It screamed a single word. *Help.*

"We're already both getting a moment on our father's arm," Aria argued. She didn't normally go out of her way to fight for what she wanted, which told me this meant something. "How stupid would it look for him to double back out of nowhere and, like, pick up the other one and walk her down the aisle? It's absurd."

"You are never going to agree on this." Sienna got up and wrapped her arms around Valentina from behind. I wouldn't normally have called my sister a peacemaker, but then it was different when she handled a situation that didn't involve me. She had a surprisingly level head on her shoulders when she wasn't acting like an annoying little sister. "And just think what an absolutely stunning impression you're going to make. Two gorgeous brides, with their handsome dad between them, with the attention of half of East Hampton on them as they walk down this wide aisle covered in flower petals. I'm actually jealous of how exquisite it's going to be."

Valentina wasn't swayed. "That sounds like a lot

of your PR talk," she scoffed, waving a hand. "This isn't an event you're trying to spin."

"I think you need to let this one go." Evan took Sienna's place, laughing softly as he hugged his fiancée. "At the end of the day, it's going to be a beautiful event, and people will be talking about it for years. And Aria is right," he added with a wink in her direction. "It will be dramatic and memorable, watching the two of you float down the aisle with Magnus between you."

"I thought my ears were burning." My uncle Magnus entered the room, smiling benevolently, finally noticing the presence of Rose and me. "There you are. Your mother will be glad," he told me.

When I raised an eyebrow, my sister explained, "You know Mom. She's got this premonition that something's going to go wrong."

"Don't even say that out loud," Rose warned as we continued into the house. "We're bringing nothing but good energy into this, everybody."

"Where is Mom?" I asked. "Did Eloise run her ragged?"

"No, Zoe got here this afternoon to watch over the kids," Valentina reminded me, referring to the nanny she and Evan used for their daughter, Isabel, who'd recently had her first birthday.

"They're upstairs having their baths if you want to pop in."

"I need to kiss my baby," Rose announced, already on her way to the stairs. I followed her, which meant the bonus of getting to stare at her ass.

One thing I often heard from married men was the thrill always died in a relationship once wedding rings were brought into the mix, especially after the addition of kids. Nothing could've been further from the truth for us. I wanted her just as much this far into our relationship as I ever had, if not more. Now, I had the honor of watching her become a mother and witnessing how she nurtured our daughter. There was nothing as satisfying. It made me crave her like a drug.

All it took was hearing Eloise giggling and splashing in the bath to change my course of thought. We found her in the tub with Isabel, with the nanny kneeling on the floor and supervising their play.

"Hi, baby!" Right away, Rose slipped off the thin cardigan she wore over a sleeveless top and kicked off her heels, kneeling in front of the tub. "Zoe, take a breather," she offered the nanny. "I can finish up here. Colton will help me."

So much for getting a quickie before dinner, the

way I had secretly hoped. I wasn't upset, though, as I rolled up my shirt sleeves. I'd been in meetings half the day, trying to button up a few last-minute plans before taking the long weekend. "Are you having fun with your best friend?" I asked my baby girl while pulling towels from the linen closet.

"Daddy! Splash!" Rose and I had to duck and cover when water flew everywhere, but it was impossible not to laugh at the sound of Eloise's sweet giggles, which got Isabel giggling with her until the sound filled the room.

"Good job, baby girl," I told her. Green eyes, so like her mother's, shone when she looked up at me, reducing me to a helpless puddle as always. Nobody ever told me it would be like this one day. If they had, I might not have been so resistant to the idea of settling down before Rose and I got together.

"It's enough to make me wonder if we shouldn't start trying for a little brother or sister," I mused, watching Rose to gauge her reaction while washing Eloise's blonde curls. It gave me the pleasure of seeing a slow smile spread across her face.

"Do you mean that?" she asked, her eyes shining with hope when they met mine. "Because I've been thinking about that for a while, myself."

Watching the girls play, I said, "It looks like we've

got this whole parenthood thing under control so far. There's plenty of room for two. I think we should go for it."

"I'm ready when you are," Rose told me just as Isabel splashed her, leaving her sputtering and blinking water out of her eyes while I tried not to laugh. "Maybe not this very minute, though."

2

COLTON

"This was a great idea." I raised my bottle of lager to Valentina, whose idea it was to have a clambake tonight. There would be enough activity over the next few days and more than enough opportunity to dress up and behave ourselves in front of guests and cameras.

Tonight, we lounged around on the beach, arranged on blankets and chairs circling the fire pit dug earlier in the day. Rose sat in my lap, now dressed as casually as I was, both of us stuffed full of seafood.

Noah, Lucian, and Evan tossed around a football while Miles chatted with Mom's cousin, Spencer, who had come from LA for the wedding. He and

Miles were on the verge of patenting some new technology. I didn't know much about it, as it wasn't my area of expertise, but they sure as hell seemed invested as they continued their conversation apart from the rest of the group.

"Am I going to get any time with you tonight?" Aria asked Miles, winding an arm around his. She shook a finger at Spencer, who chuckled when she chided, "It's not fair to monopolize one of the grooms."

"You know I would never dream of getting between a bride-to-be and her groom." He laughed, but there was something hollow in the sound. He was Mom's cousin, in his early thirties and lived it up in LA while he made his mark in the tech world.

He raked a hand through his dirty blond hair, looking down into his empty beer bottle. "I think I need a refill." He must have thought no one was looking when he slid Miles a furtive look, which hinted at a conversation that needed to be continued elsewhere.

Miles played it off, turning his full attention to Aria. "Hey, now," he teased. "You're three days away from being stuck with me forever. You can't wait five minutes for me to finish a conversation?"

"What can I say?" she asked. "I'm greedy for you." The way they looked at each other spoke volumes. It left me grinning at Rose, who touched her head to my shoulder and laced our fingers together.

"I need a glass of wine!" My Aunt Evelyn settled in a cushioned lounge chair positioned between Mom and Olivia. She wore the happy but exhausted look of a woman whose twin daughters were about to get married and had driven her crazy for the past six months of planning. "Whoever thought a double wedding was a good idea..."

Uncle Magnus stepped up behind her and placed his hands on her shoulders. "I'm pretty sure it was you. Correct me if I'm wrong."

Dad laughed from his chair on the other side of the fire. "Those are pretty bold words, you know. Haven't you learned by now you never remind a woman of the things she's said?"

"Excuse me?" Mom folded her arms, eyes narrowed. "Do you want to repeat that?"

"Spoken with love," he insisted in a light voice, laughing with Uncle Magnus.

"You want to know the secret to a long marriage?" Aunt Pepper asked, winking at us from her chair beside Uncle Connor. "It's letting your husband think you agree with him even when you know he's wrong."

"When have I ever been wrong?" Uncle Magnus asked, making us all laugh.

"Honestly," Aria interjected with a sigh once the laughter died down. "I think we've had the best possible example of what makes a good marriage."

"Agreed." Valentina jumped up from her blanket and scurried over to Uncle Magnus, throwing her arms around his waist. "Thanks to you two."

"Did you ever see it turning out this way?" Uncle Connor chuckled, a glass of scotch in his hand. "The kids growing up, getting married, tying the families closer together. It's incredible the way things unfolded."

"I still feel like I have to pinch myself," Mom admitted. "How did we become the older generation? When did that happen? I feel just as young tonight as I did on my wedding weekend."

"Even if we can't drink as much and still expect to be functional the next day," Olivia pointed out, draining what was left in her wine glass. "And I think that will be it for me. Oh, youth. Don't you kids take it for granted," she warned us.

I didn't feel so young anymore. There I was, a married man with my eighteen-month-old daughter asleep in my childhood vacation home, on the grounds of which an elaborate wedding would soon take place. One of the grooms had been my best friend since we were teenagers. Nothing about this felt real, but there was no denying it. "I'm turning into an old man," I admitted to my wife, who looked at me with wide eyes that glowed in the firelight.

"That's not true." She laughed lightly and shook her head. "Don't listen to Mom. You know how she gets at times like this. All sentimental and emotional and stuff."

I wasn't so easily convinced. "It's true, though, isn't it? We're the responsible adults now. One day, we'll be the ones sitting around a bonfire while our kids are on the verge of getting married."

"We should be so lucky." She planted a chaste kiss against my cheek, then brushed her lips against my ear, whispering, "Want to reclaim a little of your youth, Mr. Black?"

There was nothing in the world that could get me hard in an instant the way her flirtatious whisper did. "What did you have in mind?" I asked, playing dumb while fighting the thickening in my boxer briefs.

"I think I could come up with something." She glanced around like she was checking to make sure nobody was paying attention, then got up and began heading toward the house. I followed her without saying a word since nobody would ever accuse me of ruining a good thing. And when Rose got that look in her eye, it meant good things were coming.

The silence inside the house was almost deafening after hours spent talking and laughing. Rose crooked a finger, already halfway across the kitchen after entering from the back porch. "Where are we going?" I asked, caught between laughing and lusting once my attention landed on her perfect ass. It swayed hypnotically, leading me out of the kitchen and into the great room.

Once I realized she was on her way to the stairs, I jogged to catch up and take hold. "I have a better idea," I growled out and pulled her into the powder room beside the stairs instead.

"In the bathroom?" she whispered, giggling as I closed the door and flipped the lock.

"I can't wait. Besides..." I added between kisses against her neck, "... old people do it in the bedroom. A quickie in the bathroom is for young people."

Her laughter turned to a strangled whimper as I

worked my hand between her thighs to cup her pussy. I couldn't begin to count the number of times I had touched her this way, but the rush of power never changed knowing how to make her melt and beg.

My fingers flirted with the lacy edge of her thong when familiar moisture began to seep from between her swollen lips. Her mouth found mine in a hard, desperate kiss that stirred a growl in my throat and turned my cock to steel. Every stroke of her tongue, every breathless whimper sent lightning racing down my spine until nothing would do but bury myself deep inside her.

She used the counter for leverage, lifting herself and letting me yank the thong down over her feet. "We did talk about trying for another, didn't we?" she whispered as she unbuttoned my jeans and dipped a hand inside my boxer briefs. When her fingers closed around my shaft, I could barely bite back a groan. "No condom. Come inside me."

Like I would argue with that.

There was nothing playful about the way Rose guided me inside her without another word. Her head fell back, and her body went still while I sank myself into her hot, wet pussy. Every inch was better than the last until my knees shook from the sensation of being gripped from head to base with nothing between us.

"Oh, fuck..." she whispered. I could only groan in agreement, staying still to savor the thrill of being locked with her this way. Every time was like the first time. I would never get tired of it.

When her eyes opened and locked on mine, the hunger in them made me pull my hips back to drive myself in again. "You want me to put another baby in you?" I grunted, slamming home hard enough to leave her gritting her teeth. "You want me to fill this pussy?"

"Yes," she gritted out, jerking her hips to meet my strokes.

I slid my thumb against her clit to push her closer to the edge, and her fast, ragged breaths filled the small space. I covered her mouth with mine to muffle the sound, but there was nothing I could do about the vanity as it rattled from the force of our bodies crashing together.

My pace quickened, her muscles clenching around me, pulling me deeper. Her needy, high-pitched whine told me she was close, and I let myself go, her pussy drawing every drop of cum from my balls, milking me dry.

"Shit," I grunted out, leaning against her for a

second, my face against her neck. "There is nothing in the world like being bare inside you."

She chuckled softly and kissed my cheek, sighing. "After two whole years?"

"And probably after twenty years," I told her, lifting my head for a kiss.

"Hurry!"

We both looked at the locked door when we heard the sudden cry. "What the fuck?" I whispered, my mind immediately going to Eloise before my heart started racing again. There were more loud and panicked voices, overlapping while I rushed through to pull myself together.

"I'll drive!"

"You've had too much to drink. I'll drive."

"Oh, no!"

"Everything will be fine, don't worry!"

I launched myself out of the powder room to find total chaos erupting, with people running everywhere, thrusting their feet into shoes they'd taken off to go down to the beach while shouting orders and questions. "What the hell is going on?" I demanded, raising my voice over the commotion.

Ari noticed me on his way to the door, and his stricken look chilled my blood. "The store. Something happened at the store."

"What? What about the store?" Rose joined me, gripping my arm as her nails dug into my skin.

"Pumpkin, somebody from the village called Barrett." Ari looked sick, adding, "There's been a fire."

That was all I needed to hear to get me moving, taking Rose by the hand and pulling her along when it seemed like she was frozen in place. Shock would do that to a person.

"Stay here with the kids!" I ordered Zoe, who stood wide-eyed on the stairs. At least they were asleep and didn't have to witness their parents' frenzy.

We were just there. How could this have happened? Questions slammed around inside my skull as I rushed out to the car and placed Rose inside. She was wide-eyed and mute—the way a person would react when they found out something they gave their life to was in danger of being destroyed. I could only hope the destruction was minimal as I pulled out, falling in place behind Noah's car as we all drove down to get a look for ourselves.

As it turned out, there was no getting anywhere

near the scene in a car. I settled for pulling into a spot two blocks away from the fire trucks and caution tape, barely taking time to put the car in park before following Rose as she sprinted toward the crowd growing behind the yellow tape.

Acrid smoke hung heavy in the air, and the thought of what that smoke represented was almost too much to comprehend. We were just there, dammit.

Firefighters trained water on the remains of what only hours ago was a beautiful, historic building. When I thought back on the pains we took to keep the building's original charm intact, it was enough to lodge a lump in my throat. This was my first job, my way of proving myself to Dad, showing him I could be trusted to handle a project of size and importance.

And it was gone.

There was nothing left but cinders. "How the fuck did it all go up like that?" Dad's question went unanswered, almost swallowed by the overlapping questions and pained groans coming from all around us.

Especially from Rose. "Oh my God," she whimpered. I had never heard anyone sound so beaten. So destroyed. She had to turn away from the destruction, gripping my polo in her fists with her face pressed to my chest. "Oh my God. It's all gone."

It sure as hell looked that way from where we stood. This project brought us together, and now there was nothing left of it but burnt timber.

"We can rebuild," I assured her, rubbing her back. "Nothing is lost forever. We'll build it again."

"How could this have happened?" she asked in a voice thick with tears.

"The dresses!" Aunt Evelyn's heartbroken wail pierced the air while Aunt Pepper cried on Uncle Connor's shoulder. "God, what if someone was in there?"

Her question made me look toward the twins, hugging each other and weeping. Magnus tried to comfort them, but he didn't have much more luck than their fiancés did. "We'll figure it out," he offered while he exchanged a worried look with Dad, who comforted Mom as best he could.

"These things happen," Dad murmured, but it was clear there was nothing to be said. The fact was, we were all shaken by what we saw in front of us.

"What the hell happened to the sprinkler system?" Olivia demanded, though there was no one around to provide an answer. It was a question I would've liked to have answered too.

For the time being, all I could do was try to comfort my wife, whose heartbroken sobs threatened to tear my heart from my chest. "What are we going to do?" she asked. "We lost everything inside. We lost the wedding dresses. What do we do now?"

If only I had an answer.

3

———

NOAH

The second my eyes opened the morning after the fire, I would've sworn I smelled smoke.

Two days until the so-called *Wedding of the Decade,* and the brides had nothing to wear. They had spent hours crying last night, with all of us gathered together in the great room to comfort them.

Amazing how quickly things had changed from the happy, almost hectic energy before dinner.

We had only fallen asleep after showering, where we washed our hair twice to get rid of the stench of smoke, then collapsed into bed. Sienna was too heartsick for anything else, and I couldn't pretend the fire hadn't shaken me, hearing the girls cry, not to mention our moms, mine included.

"Are you awake?" I barely heard Sienna's sleepy mumble, half-muffled by the pillow she'd bunched up under her head. She had her back to me with a sheet loosely draped over her bare body. How many times had I seen her this way? And she never failed to make my dick stir.

"How did you know without looking?" I asked, running a finger down her back. So perfect, all mine.

"Your breathing changed." She rolled over, her body half covering mine. Her thick, dark hair puddled on my chest while she sought my kiss. "You think I don't have every part of you cataloged, Goldsmith?"

"You make me sound like a work project." I kissed her forehead, nose, and fingertips once she finished running a hand down my cheek.

Her laughter was soft, sexy. "We've already done that, remember?" she whispered, sliding her leg over mine and conjuring up all kinds of ideas. "Look where it got us."

"Are you complaining?" I took her left hand in mine, admiring the sparkling diamond ring that had taken me weeks to choose. There I was, the man at the head of a real estate empire, someone who regularly made multi-million-dollar decisions, unable to decide which ring my fiancée would like the best.

Ever the ballbuster, she replied, "Not yet."

Her smirk faded fast, though, once she noticed the clock on the nightstand. "Damn. Aren't you guys supposed to be on the yacht by nine? It's quarter to eight. We'd better get moving."

"I guess so." Colton had chartered a yacht with the idea of the guys going fishing. I had to wonder whether anyone would feel like fishing after last night, but sitting around feeling shitty wouldn't change anything. "And I guess you girls will…"

She wrinkled her nose. "Look for dresses and hope there's something suitable. Yeah. Pretty much." Rolling away, she added, "Wait a second. I almost forgot."

I hated watching her do this, but it wouldn't be much longer before we could tell everybody the good news. It didn't seem right, making the announcement now, stealing focus from the people who mattered most this weekend.

She slid the platinum and diamond ring over her finger, reaching over me to nestle it snuggly in the velvet-lined box on the nightstand. "I can't wait to show everybody," she murmured, smiled at the ring, then turned that smile on me.

How did I ever live without her? How did I live without this? Something as simple as brushing her long, dark locks over her shoulder so I could press my lips to the bare skin I revealed. It was warm and soft, and it carried the scent of her perfume. Something by Dior which she could wear forever as far as I was concerned. I would have bought her a lifetime supply if I didn't know it would lose its scent over time.

Her smile didn't last long. "It won't be easy trying to stay happy and positive today." With her hand on my chest, she propped her chin on top, sighing.

I ran my fingers through her hair, something that always calmed her. "It's not your responsibility to keep everybody happy," I gently reminded her. I didn't want to seem cold, like I didn't care. Nothing could have been further from the truth. I wouldn't make a big deal about it, but I was just as shaken by what we found in the village last night as she was. A reminder that everything could go up in smoke at any time. We were lucky. We could replace whatever we lost.

But some things couldn't be replaced, could they? That store represented a hell of a lot of work for Colton, and now it was gone along with the gowns Aria and Valentina had chosen to wear on the biggest day of their lives. It fucking sucked, putting it mildly, and of course, it would put a damper on the whole event.

"What do you think you'll do? Go back to the city?" I asked, still combing my fingers through her hair, noticing how her eyes slowly closed, and a look of satisfaction softened her frown.

"I heard your dad say something last night about having assistants bring out whatever they could pull from storage for the sake of finding something new. The bridesmaids' dresses, I'm not as worried about," she confessed. "There were other choices we liked just as much. But the bridal gowns were one-of-a-kind. It's heartbreaking."

"I know. But trust me," I told her, trying to smile for her sake. "They have a shit ton of dresses to choose from. Dad would move Heaven and Earth to make sure the twins have what they need, and you know Magnus would pay anything for extra seamstresses to do the alterations. It'll be fine. What's a wedding without a little drama?"

"Don't you dare say that." She gave my chest a soft, playful slap. "It's going to be our turn sometime, right? I don't want any drama."

"We'll have the most boring wedding in the history of weddings," I promised, kissing her forehead. "Guests will be falling asleep during the ceremony."

"Shut up!" She was giggling as I rolled her over, kissing her neck, groping whatever I could reach.

"We were supposed to be getting up, weren't we?" she reminded me while draping a leg over mine, pulling me closer to her heat.

"Yeah, and somebody's up." Taking her hand, I closed it around my stiff cock. Her touch was electric, sending ripples of heat through me and turning desire into desperate, panting need with every stroke.

"But I thought we were in a hurry..." She loved to tease me, and of course, she would choose a moment like this when I was rock hard and looking to bury my dick in her to play innocent.

"I'm still in a hurry," I confessed, thrusting into her fist, savoring the feel of her touch. "My priorities have shifted, is all."

"Oh, really? And what do you think you're going to do now?" She couldn't continue to play games when I pulled her nipple between my lips, rolling my tongue around it in slow circles until she arched her back and purred like a kitten. She was no match for me when I knew exactly how and where to touch her.

I had cataloged everything about her too—how much pressure and when to back off a little to draw out her pleasure. It was a point of pride—a personal goal—playing her body the way a master played his instrument.

"Just like that..." She sighed, running her fingers through my hair, holding my head in place. "God, you make me so wet."

My cock surged, and I groaned when the pressure was almost too much to handle. "That's because I know what your pussy needs," I reminded her, turning my attention to the other nipple, going back and forth so she was writhing, legs spread in silent offering.

Lifting my head, I gazed down the length of her body as I pulled the sheet away. She was nothing short of perfection, smooth and glowing in the morning sun. We both shuddered as I indulged in her silky skin, running my hand over her thigh until I reached the curve of her ass. Goose bumps rose at my touch and she shivered, whimpering softly as I draped her leg over my shoulder.

I could smell her arousal, and my lips hadn't even touched her glistening mound. Her pretty pussy was neatly shaved, her juices already flowing, leaving a small wet spot on the sheet. "What am I going to do with all of this?" I growled, inhaling deeply, pulling her essence into my lungs. I needed her, all of her, all the time. There was no life without this, without her.

"You got me wet," she reasoned with a throaty, breathless chuckle. "You should clean me up."

"What do you know? I was thinking the same thing." Our eyes met for one long, silent moment before I descended, delved through her folds, used my tongue to part her lips, and lapped up every drop of her exquisite nectar.

"Oh God!" She gasped, hips lifting as her body took over, demanding what it needed. I gave it to her just the way she liked it, running my tongue over her clit, flicking the tip until her breathing went harsh, frantic. That was my cue to slow down—her frustrated whine didn't do her any favors.

"Let me come," she whispered, pulled my head closer, and ground her pussy against my face.

She knew better than that. All it would get her was more frustration since I slowed to the point my tongue barely moved. I gazed across her body, past her heaving tits, and into her blazing eyes. "Let me come," she begged.

Her head hit the pillow, and she growled louder when I shook my head, chuckling, then I went back to work. I was in no hurry now, not when she was writhing and needy like this. My kickass, brilliant fiancée who took shit from nobody was begging me like her life depended on it. Everything else could wait.

As usual, she found a way to turn the tables. "At least let me suck your dick while you do this," she suggested, pushing herself up on her elbows.

Now, that got my attention. There wasn't much else in the world that could have convinced me to lift my head away from her sweet aroma. "If you insist..." I rolled onto my back, my dick dripping with excitement that only got more intense when Sienna hovered over my face, inches from my mouth. I took her hips in my hands and pulled her down so I could thrust my tongue inside her dripping cunt.

"Oh, fuck yes." She sighed. The touch of her tongue to my swollen head wiped out all conscious thought. There was nothing to do but feel her mouth sliding down the length of my shaft. She massaged me with her tongue while I fucked her with mine, groping her ass, reaching between us to fondle her tits while her head bobbed.

I couldn't keep up with the sensations as all of my senses were assaulted—smell, taste, hearing, and touch. It wasn't easy to focus on what I was doing to her while she expertly worked my cock, increased the pressure, and used her hand to cover what her mouth couldn't take.

It was when she started to grind, hard and determined, that I knew she was getting close. "You're so good to my cock," I whispered, replacing my tongue with a pair of fingers which I slid deep into her dripping heat, quivering hole. The slightest brush against her G-spot made her cry out around me, bearing down and sucking harder.

"That's right," I urged, finger fucking her tight pussy while she writhed and moaned. "A good girl gets to come the way she wants to. Is that what you want? You want to come for me?"

She released me, gasping, as she whispered, "Yes! Yes, so close… just like that…" She pushed back against me faster until a rush of fresh warmth coated my knuckles, and she came until her legs shook. All I could do was hold on, lost in fascination at the sight of what I could do to her.

But there was still the matter of my very hard, aching dick to deal with. "Now," I ordered, caressed her ass and gave it a slap. "See what you can do with my cock inside you. Let me watch you ride me."

There was no better sight in the world. Nothing I

craved more than watching her fall apart with me inside her. She wasted no time, turning around and throwing a shaky leg over me. "I love you," she breathed out, staring deep into my eyes as she guided me into her tight, welcoming heat.

"Fuck, yeah." I ran my hands over her, intoxicated at the feel of her warm body while her tight pussy gripped me, milking and inviting me to fill her.

I watched, entranced as her head fell back, mouth hung open in pure, mindless bliss. She set a slow, sensual rhythm, rolled her hips while her pussy gripped every inch of me and sent a shudder down my spine. It wasn't enough to watch her firm tits swing. I had to take them in my hands, both of us groaning when she picked up her pace.

"That's it. Ride my cock." I groaned, thrusted upward, and watched between us as I disappeared inside her again and again. "Fuck, baby. Taking my cock so good," I praised, pulled her onto me, and ground her against me. "Make yourself come. I want to feel you dripping around me. Show me how you need it."

"Mmm... Noah," she whispered, leaned on my chest, and ground her clit against my base. "So close... it's so good."

"Give it to me." My hands slid over her ass, up her back, while her whimpers turned to something more—high-pitched as she rocked her hips faster until she went still and gripped me so tight my teeth ground together.

I couldn't hold back, not that I wanted to, and let myself follow her into oblivion. Shockwaves rolled over me, and pleasure radiated through my limbs until I went as limp as Sienna, who was now draped on top of me in a breathless heap.

"Well..." She released a soft laugh that made her breath fan across my sweat-damp skin. "That's a good way to start the day. I might be able to get through it with a genuinely positive attitude after coming like that."

"I aim to please." Her thick hair slid through my fingers when I brushed it away from her face to kiss her. "And everything will turn out fine. Keep reminding yourself of that. In the end, the fire won't be anything but a footnote."

"One day, we'll look back on this and laugh," she mused with a smirk. "Right?"

"Something like that, smart-ass." I smacked the ass in question, easing her off me. "Now, we need to get moving. I don't need Colton barging in here, wanting to know why I'm holding up the excursion he planned."

Sienna only snorted and rolled away with a soft laugh. "He's acting more and more like Dad all the time. Don't tell him I said that."

"Don't worry," I assured her on my way to the shower. "I'll save it for the next time he needs his balls busted and pretend it came from me."

4

NOAH

The mood downstairs was about as cheerful as a funeral. I couldn't shake the sense of walking on eggshells as Sienna and I wandered hand in hand into the kitchen, where the aroma of coffee promised the pick-me-up we all desperately needed.

Rose sat in the breakfast nook overlooking the back porch and the beach beyond it. Tomorrow, a team would descend onto the area to prepare it for the wedding. It was clear from the scowl she wore that she wasn't interested in the scenery, typing furiously on her phone. She didn't bother saying good morning, settling for a soft grunt in response to my greeting. Her eyes never left the screen.

Colton was at the counter, fixing two plates from the breakfast buffet that had been laid out. When I looked his way, he gave his head a slight shake. A lifetime of knowing each other was enough to explain what he meant. *Don't bother. Not right now.* He then set a plate of fruit and a yogurt parfait in front of Rose, who only grunted again.

"Spencer just came in from his run on the beach," Colton explained. "He'll be down soon. The others?"

That was something I hadn't thought about until now. Spencer could get up at the crack of dawn for a run. He didn't have a worried partner to sit up with last night.

The parents were out on the porch, drinking their coffee, deep in conversation. Dad noticed me watching and waved me outside. I took my coffee with me and stepped out into a cool, breezy morning. Seagulls sailed over the sparkling water, and gentle waves lapped at the shore. It was idyllic except for the worried looks worn by Mom and aunts.

"I have an entire truck full of sample dresses on the way up to the house," Dad told me. "I thought I could have a lunch set up for everyone by the time you boys come back from your fishing trip. Ideally, the girls will be able to greet you happily when you arrive." His fingers were crossed when he raised them.

"That's a good idea," I agreed, glimpsing at Rose through the window. Her head was bent, her shoulders almost touching her ears while she continued typing. "Anything to pick up the mood."

"That's what I was going for," he agreed. His reflection in the glass told me he was watching her too. "She's doing everything she can to mitigate the fallout from this. There were a handful of customers with pieces waiting to be picked up from the store. We'll need to issue a press release, too, letting people know the East Hampton location will be out of commission for the foreseeable future."

People would probably find out about it through word of mouth just as easily, but I settled for agreeing, "Sure. Can I help somehow?"

He offered a sincere smile that faded as he shook his head. "Unless you can find a way to help your sister through this. It shook her badly."

"Sienna will do her best to pick things up," I predicted, watching her slide into a chair next to Rose. It was obvious she was trying to cheer her up, to at least take her mind off things for a minute. And it was apparent she wasn't successful.

I couldn't hear them, but body language spoke volumes. Rose tried to be polite but was too distracted to play along. It was enough to make me consider announcing our engagement, if only to pick up everybody's spirits for a little while. I decided to leave the idea in my back pocket, just in case.

Mom joined us and touched a hand to my shoulder. "Somebody has to start smiling around here," she murmured, standing on tiptoe to kiss my cheek. "It will be good for you to get out there on the water. You'll have something else to think about."

"We'll be fine," I promised. "And I know that building had to be insured to the hilt, right?"

"Of course," Dad assured me, almost waving the idea off like it wasn't worth thinking about. "All of that is taken care of. We can rebuild."

As I watched, Miles entered the kitchen, leading Aria by the hand. Either she hadn't bothered putting on makeup to cover the circles under her eyes, or she had tried, and this was the best she'd managed. Sienna shot a worried look my way, and I murmured, "I'll head back in, see what I can do."

The problem was, I couldn't imagine what. Aria did everything she could to keep a brave face, but her chin trembled enough to tell me she was still wrecked after last night. As I walked back into the house, Sienna gathered her in a tight hug. "We've got you, girl," she vowed, meeting my gaze over Aria's shoulder. "Your wedding is still going to be amazing."

Aria's soft laugh was a little shaky. "I know. At least, I need to believe it." She offered me a brief, weak grin, asking, "The dress is just one aspect of the day, right?"

"There you go. That's the spirit." Evelyn was behind them, telling me she had probably given Aria a pep talk before they came down from the guest room. There was strain around her eyes, which looked a little puffy like it wasn't only the girls who cried last night. Weddings tended to do that to people. Months of dreaming meant it hurt unfathomably worse when something like this happened.

"You get to spend the day trying on more pretty gowns," Sienna pointed out. "It'll be fun. Like a big game of dress-up. You know there's going to be a zillion beautiful, gorgeous gowns to choose from."

"I know. It'll be fine." Aria's jaw tightened like she was trying to convince herself.

Miles surprised me by looking just as haunted as his bride. "You all right?" I asked and gripped his shoulder once Aria gave in and let Evelyn fix her a plate of food. Sienna followed them, leaving us with Colton on the other side of the spacious room.

When we were more or less out of earshot of the girls, he blew out a deep breath. "A bit zonked," he confessed, running a hand over the back of his neck and sighing. There were still times after two years spent exclusively in the States when he'd come out with British slang. "We had a long night. But I have no right to complain compared to the way she must feel. I can't tell you how many times she said she couldn't wait for me to see her dress."

"Everything will turn out fine," I predicted, watching as Aria attempted to be cheerful. Then I looked around, counting heads. "Who are we missing?"

"Not us." Evan sounded overly bright as he entered the room as if he was trying a little too hard. I gave him a sympathetic grimace before Valentina appeared behind him. She looked a lot like her sister this morning, though the circles under her eyes weren't quite as dark.

"So it's Spencer and Lucian we're waiting for?" Colton checked the time, heading out to the foyer. A few seconds later, his voice rang out loud enough to make us all wince. "We're going to be late for the yacht! What's the holdup?"

Valentina went straight to Aria and gave her a bear hug, letting out a soft, determined grunt. "Okay, so our gowns went up in smoke," she announced, sounding like the same bossy, type-A girl she had always been. "Big deal. Everything's going to be perfect otherwise, right?"

"Right," Aria agreed with a bright, strained smile. It was almost like they were trying to convince themselves, and I had to give them credit for trying their hardest.

Sienna clapped her hands briskly, then placed them on her hips. "No more feeling sorry for ourselves. Anybody." I noticed the anxious way she eyed Rose when she added, "We have a lot to do this weekend, and now this is just one more thing to get out of the way. Let's not drag our feet."

"Listen to you." Colton shook his head slowly as he rejoined us, grinning at his sister. "I didn't know you decided to play drill sergeant this weekend."

She tossed her hair back from her shoulders, shrugging. "Somebody's got to keep everybody in line, right? It shouldn't have to be the bride's responsibility, so I took the job."

A loud sniffle drew everybody's attention, and we

turned to find Rose running a hand under her eyes. "I'm sorry," she mumbled, shaking her head. "It's just that I don't know if I can forgive myself if this was somehow my fault. What if I left something plugged in that shouldn't have been? Or I might have overloaded an outlet without realizing it."

I was standing closest so I went to her and crouched by her side. "Hey. Don't do this to yourself, sis. The fire chief will have a report, right? I'm sure it was a random accident, that's all. You are the most conscientious person I know."

All that got me was a bitter laugh. "Apparently not this time." She was damn determined to heap all the blame on her shoulders, stubborn as always. I looked at Colton, silently wondering what I could say that might help.

It was Sienna who came up with something on the fly. "We're engaged," she announced in a loud, clear voice.

So much for keeping it to ourselves.

The room went deadly silent for a heartbeat before Rose let out a dramatic gasp and swiveled in her chair, her blue eyes wide when they landed on me. "Is that true? You got engaged?" she asked, taking me by the shoulders. "And you didn't tell anybody?"

"When the hell did it happen?" Colton asked. "Holy shit!"

Miles barked out a laugh. "Why didn't you say anything?"

"When were you going to tell us?" Valentina demanded while Aria squealed, bounced on the balls of her feet, and threw her arms around Sienna.

"I'm absolutely chuffed," Aria told her, then burst out laughing. "Listen to me. I sound like Miles now," she added, mimicking his British accent.

"When were you going to tell your parents?" Evelyn almost shrieked as she threw her hands into the air. "And don't tell me either of your mothers could keep something like that a secret."

I exchanged looks with my fiancée, who shrugged. The fact that we both had the same thought shouldn't have come as a surprise. It was almost unnerving how in sync we were sometimes. "We didn't want to steal the focus this weekend," I explained as Rose threw her arms around me.

"I'm so happy for you! Oh my God!" Just as suddenly, she let go long enough to slap my shoulder. "And you can't tell your own sister? You're saying even Mom and Dad don't know?"

"Nobody knows," Sienna explained. Her eyes sparkled, and she bit down on her lip before she said, "Hold on! Let me go up and get my ring! I've been dying to show you!"

"I want to see it right away!" Rose took off behind her, followed by the twins. Their excited chatter was music to my ears. If there was one thing Sienna understood, it was people, what they needed to hear, when they needed to hear it. That quality made her perfect for PR, but just then, I couldn't help but reflect on how it made her perfect for me.

"I'm calling everybody inside!" Evelyn hurried to the door, beaming. "We'll have to open some champagne to celebrate!"

"I don't think we have time for that," I said, but she didn't hear me or didn't feel like listening.

Colton was the first to shake my hand. "Don't worry about the schedule. This deserves a toast."

"Man, congratulations." Evan's head swung back and forth between Colton and me. "It wasn't enough for one of you to marry the other one's sister? You both have to do it?"

"Honestly," Miles admitted. "We were wondering how long it would take you to sack up and pop the question."

"Who is we?" I asked with a laugh, looking around at the group. "You have nothing better to do than lay odds on how long it'll take a guy to propose to his girlfriend?"

"You did what?" Mom barely paused in the doorway leading to the porch. She raised her sunglasses and gaped at me for a second before she flew toward me with her arms outstretched. "I don't know whether I want to hug you or strangle you for not telling us!"

She went with the hug as everybody else poured into the kitchen, and soon, we went through another round of handshakes just as Sienna came in from the foyer with her left hand held high. "Surprise!" she shouted.

This was what I had looked forward to—watching her soak in the love from the people who mattered to her the most. They gathered around to admire the ring, hug her, and basically give her the same sort of shit they gave me for keeping things quiet.

"I only proposed last week," I explained while nudging my way through the crowd. "It's not like we've been planning the wedding for months without mentioning it."

"I'm breaking out the champagne," Mom announced as she wiped her eyes. "You kids. I'll be crying my eyes out all weekend at this rate."

"How did you propose?" Rose asked, sliding an arm around Colton's waist and resting her head against his chest. For the first time since we hung out on the beach last night, she looked like her usual, happy self.

"The way a person usually does," I replied, playing dumb. "One knee, ring in a box."

She groaned the way only a little sister could. "I can see why you said yes," she told Sienna, who giggled.

"No, really." The ring sparkled when Sienna placed her hand on my chest. Was she wiggling her finger a little to make the diamond catch the light? Possibly. She had waited an entire week for this and was going to soak up every second. "It was amazing. Noah made up a story about wanting me to look at a property he was looking to purchase in Chicago and flew us out on his company jet. It was all a big charade. He took me to the most gorgeous restaurant for dinner. Then, we took a moonlight boat ride on Lake Michigan. That was when he popped the question."

"You did a great job with the ring, for sure." Mom nudged Sienna, beaming. "I raised him right."

"No arguments here," Sienna agreed. "I think I'll keep him."

"Wait a second." Evelyn paused in the middle of handing out the champagne. "Where are Lucian and Ivy? We can't make a toast without them."

"Oh, no." Sienna covered her face with one hand while she laughed. "We have to go through all of this again! I should've waited until they got down here to blurt it out."

Leaning down, I whispered, "It was perfect. Like you."

5

LUCIAN

"Lucian."

Fuck me. Nobody had ever spoken my name the way Ivy did. She turned it into a song. A prayer she repeated like a litany as I worked my way in and out of her, giving her all of me.

She curled my wet hair around her fingers, holding my head close to her neck. Warm breath tickled my ear before her tongue danced over the lobe. "Lucian," she rasped as she moved with me, sliding up and down the tile wall.

"So good," I gritted out, fighting the urge to let go. The temptation was almost too much—the promise of release and losing myself in this woman who had given me everything worth possessing. "Fuck, Poison. You feel so good."

"The feeling of you inside me, it's..." She trailed off, her head falling back. I pressed my mouth to her throat, took it as the offering it was, and felt how her pulse pounded under my tongue, the vibrations of every moan, every sigh.

It was like two of us becoming one. I didn't know where my body stopped and hers began. I only knew I needed more of whatever this was. I needed it for the rest of my life.

She opened her eyes and looked into mine, her gray orbs swirling with lust and pleasure. "I love it when your cock is buried deep inside me," she whispered, thrusting her tongue inside my mouth in a deep, all-consuming kiss that almost made me forget to move. Her teeth grazed my bottom lip, then she sucked it hard, drawing a long groan out of me as I slammed into her again.

"Oh, God," she breathed out, dragging her nails over my back, the sting from the water making me groan through my teeth. I thrust into her harder, driving deep the way I knew she needed it—the way we both did.

"Yes... *yes*... f-fuck me, Lucian." She held my head

close and whispered in my ear, "Harder. I-I I'm almost…"

She didn't need to tell me. I knew she was almost there, her cunt clenched around me as she sank her teeth into my shoulder. "Let go," I growled out, almost crushing her between me and the wall with every unforgiving stroke. She let out a high-pitched whimper between helpless gasps, and I relished her sounds of pleasure—pleasure I was giving her. "Let me feel you fall apart around me. Cream on my cock, Poison."

"I… oh fuck… Lucian!" She bit my shoulder again at the last second, stifling what would've been deafening in the shower stall otherwise. The tingle in my spine and the heaviness of my balls wouldn't be ignored. I closed my eyes, letting go, filling her.

By the time I finished, my ears were ringing, while Ivy's breathless whimpers faded until she let out a soft chuckle and touched her mouth to my sore muscle. "Sorry," she whispered, kissing the spot where her teeth had dug in hard. "I don't know what got into me."

"Last I checked, it was my dick," I reminded her. She only rolled her eyes at my corny joke, then sighed in what sounded like disappointment when I slid out of her pussy. I understood the feeling all too well. There was always a sense of loss when I left her.

Without saying a word, I pulled the showerhead down from the mount and trained it on her sensitive flesh. She leaned against the wall again, eyes closed while I cleaned her up. "We're going to have to hurry now," she whispered, running her fingers through my wet, tangled dark hair. "I hope nobody minds us being so late."

"I doubt anybody will." Who wanted to follow a rigid schedule at a time like this, anyway? I never did understand that. An itinerary was one thing, but filling every minute with activities? Especially with the mood everybody was probably going to be after last night. I would just as soon have skipped out on fishing.

"Either way, we better move. I need to try on more dresses today with everybody else. It's such a shame." She sighed. It wasn't the first time she'd said it since we stood in silent shock along with everybody else last night, staring at what used to be an impressive storefront.

Once I finished cleaning her up, she rewarded me with a deep, long kiss that almost made me consider going back for round two. The refractory period was a real thing, though, so I settled for kissing her back and returning the showerhead to its place. "Come on, if you can walk," I teased, earning a laugh.

We wasted no time drying off, and instead of taking the time to dry her hair, Ivy opted to rub the towel over it, then clipped the nearly platinum locks in place. "If anybody asks, we overslept," she whispered after we finished getting ready, and even though it was only us in the bedroom, she blushed. "I mean, your parents are down there. Hell, my *boss* is down there."

"I'm sure Dad doesn't think of himself as your boss all the time. I mean, after us being together for two years? Besides..." I reminded her as we left the guest room at the far end of the east wing, "... last time I checked, we're not working right now."

"You know what I mean. It's weird." She was still a good girl at heart and always would be. Put her in a conference room in front of a team, and she was tough as nails. Woe to anyone, man or woman, who thought they could intimidate her into silence. Yet, put her in a real-world situation like facing her boyfriend's parents, and she turned into a blushing virgin.

With a grin, I said, "I hate to tell you, but as far as I'm concerned, we have a lifetime of that to look forward to. And I'm not going celibate anytime soon." She was giggling when I pulled her close for a quick kiss before we descended the winding staircase.

A lifetime. There was a point in my past when I would have choked on the word. I couldn't have imagined tying myself down, even after witnessing the commitment between my parents—unusual in our world, where marriages so often broke or were only an act presented to the public. Yet, from the beginning, it was clear to me that Ivy was it. That finding 'the one' was more than a myth pushed by the wedding industry. We'd talked so many times about our future like it was a done deal—one of those things two people understand instinctively.

At the sound of laughter coming from the kitchen, Ivy pulled me up short in the foyer. "What's going on?" she whispered. It sounded like everybody was in there, friends and family, parents, the entire group. And it was deafening. I shrugged, took her by the hand, and lead the way.

"There you are!" Mom shook her head at me when we reached the group. For some reason, she was holding a glass of champagne. Everybody was.

"What did we miss?" I asked, looking around

while my Aunt Lourde thrust a champagne flute into my hand.

"We're not going through the whole song and dance again." Sienna laughed. She was beaming, clearly over the moon with happiness. "Long story short, we're engaged."

Ivy let out a screech, grabbing Sienna's hand to ogle the diamond solitaire sparkling on it. "Are you kidding? When? This is amazing!"

I turned to Noah, who lifted a shoulder. "We weren't going to tell anybody, but it seemed like the right time." Clearly, he was right. I had expected everything to be dull and depressing this morning, but instead, there were happy tears and smiles.

"This is so terrific." There were tears in Ivy's eyes when she looked up from Sienna's ring. "I am so, so happy for you."

If she only knew. But no, that would go against the point of keeping it a secret. My thoughts went to the box sitting in my safe at home. A box that had sat there for months, ever since we started planning the trip to Europe in July. I had been thinking about proposing for ages, practically since we first got together as a couple. I had known she was the one for a long time, no question about it. I couldn't imagine life any other way.

Was she thinking about us now as she pumped Sienna for the details of Noah's proposal? Was she wondering if our time would ever come? It was almost enough to make me want to end her torment and ask her then and there, but she deserved the whole thing. Me on one knee in a romantic situation. She deserved the fantasy.

"I hate to break this up, but we do have somebody waiting for us at the marina." Colton patted me on the back on his way past, muttering close to my ear, "Maybe next time, wake up a little earlier so you can get off without holding us up."

"Fuck off," I replied, laughing as I shoved him out of my way so I could grab something quick to eat from the counter.

"Sorry to have missed the festivities," Spencer announced, jogging down the stairs as we entered the foyer. "I had a few calls to make. Thursday is still a workday for a lot of people," he pointed out with a sigh. I happened to look his way in time to notice the troubled glance he exchanged with Miles. Like there was something unspoken between them. Come to think of it, they had been doing a lot of that since last night. I'd forgotten about it since the fire happened.

After that, I couldn't help but pay closer attention to Miles as I went through the motions of participating once we were on the yacht, baiting my hook and busting balls with everybody else the way we normally did.

The whole time, though, I noticed how quiet Miles was. Nerves? Cold feet? Maybe, but why would Spencer have anything to do with it? Unless Miles had confided in him, which he might've done, seeing as how they weren't as close as he was with the rest of us. Sometimes, it was easier to unload on a warm acquaintance rather than on a close friend.

After an hour of observing his strange, stand-offish attitude, there was no staying quiet. "Are you okay?" I asked him as we settled in with our rods, the yacht bobbing peacefully on the gentle ripples. The sun beat down on us, but it was pleasant rather than harsh, and the presence of a fully stocked bar had everybody in a good mood.

Everybody but him, it seemed. "Everything's going to be all right," I offered, in case that was what was on his mind. I wanted to give him the benefit of the doubt. I didn't want to think he was holding something back from us.

"Sure it will be," he replied, and I had the feeling the words came out without any forethought. He wasn't really listening, just like he didn't see anything in front of him as he sat with his fishing rod in hand, staring over the water.

I decided to join in on busting Noah's balls for a while instead, laughing at his story of almost dropping the ring in Lake Michigan when he proposed. Even Spencer laughed with us, though Miles barely chuckled.

Leaning in and lowering my voice, I asked, "What's going on?" With a glance toward everybody else to make sure they were occupied, I muttered, "It's obvious there's a problem."

"Of course there is." Miles lifted a shoulder, wearing a smirk. "We were all there last night. We saw what happened. Aria is devastated, and there's not much I can do about it, but I hope she finds a new dress she loves enough to make her happy."

"I'm not talking about the fire."

He arched an eyebrow. "What are you talking about?"

"Come on," I urged. "I know you and I haven't known each other as long as the rest of us have, but it's been a couple of years now. I'm not blind. I know what it looks like when you're not yourself."

He followed the direction my attention shifted to, and we both watched as Spencer poured himself a drink at the bar rather than waiting for one of the staff. For the first time, it hit me that any stranger could look at us and imagine Miles and Spencer were related, with their dirty blond hair and light-colored eyes so unlike the dark looks I shared with my cousin and friends. "Is everything going okay with this patent you two are working on? Because every time you guys are talking, it looks like you're ready to rip each other's heads off or throw up. Either way."

"We're fine. Really." Everything about his body language screamed the opposite. His hunched shoulders, the way he clenched his jaw, the jerky way he reeled in his line.

After another few moments, he sighed, angled himself toward me and turned away from the group. The stony, blank mask dropped away. His brows knitted together over the frame of his sunglasses. "I was going to approach you about this later. Tonight, maybe."

I glanced over his shoulder to where the guys were now talking about baseball. Spencer was a Dodgers fan, which, of course, earned nothing but scorn from a bunch of diehard Yankees fans. "We can still talk later," I offered. "After we get back if you want. We don't have to wait."

"That would be good." Some of the tension

drained from his shoulders, which now lowered to a more normal position. "And for now... keep it between us, would you?"

"Of course. Don't worry about it."

He nodded firmly and turned around. A change came over him when he did. It reminded me of how he had convinced us that he was nothing but a good guy with good intentions when we first met him. Over the course of two years, the rest of the story had eventually come to light. As it turned out, he had entered our lives with the intention of destroying Magnus, Evelyn, and the twins after being fed lies virtually since birth. It had taken falling in love with Aria and learning the truth behind his late mother's lies to turn him around.

He had proven from the beginning that he was able to compartmentalize in a way that probably helped a lot when it came to business. He had to be cold as ice, able to conceal his thoughts under an expressionless façade at the drop of a hat.

Me, on the other hand? I wasn't nearly as skilled. I spent the rest of the morning and early afternoon wondering what the hell he was hiding and whether whatever it was would end up biting Aria in the ass. I hadn't known about his intentions when he first came to town from London, so there hadn't been a reason for me to feel protective of one of the girls I had grown up with.

Now? Knowing what he was capable of and he was due to marry Aria in a couple of days made me look at him through new eyes. I must've managed to play off my concerns well enough since nobody seemed to notice.

It was lunchtime by the time we docked and disembarked in the boathouse at the rear of the Goldsmith estate. We crossed the beach, and voices floated our way from high up on the terrace. One in particular left me in a hurry to get up there.

How fortunate was I that I could recognize the woman I loved just by hearing her laugh? She did so much of it that I would know the sound anywhere.

"Laughter is a good sign," Colton pointed out as we walked up the long flight of stairs leading from the beach. "I didn't get any emergency texts, so I'm hoping that means everything went well."

"Either way, I plan on telling Valentina she looks incredible in whatever Ari was able to dig up. Not that she wouldn't," Evan added. "She could wear a shower curtain for all I care. She would look just as good."

"Wow..." Noah snickered behind us. "I don't know if I can handle all this romance in the air. You better be careful, or I might just want your cock soon too.”

“Shut the fuck up,” Evan fired back over his shoulder. “You know what I mean.”

I knew I did. We were halfway up the steps when I blurted it out. “I’m proposing to Ivy when I take her to Europe next month. In Paris, specifically.”

Evan gave me a light punch on my shoulder. “Wait. Seriously?”

Everybody stopped, even Spencer. “I don’t know what made me say that,” I admitted with a laugh when all eyes were on me. “But yeah. I bought the ring. I have it all planned.”

“Shit,” Spencer murmured. “It’s like a contagious disease around here. I’m glad I’m flying home Sunday afternoon, or I might end up engaged.”

“That’s great news.” Colton was the first to shake my hand, laughing off Spencer’s joke like we all did. “How are you going to do it?”

“Now I wish I hadn’t said anything.” I ran through my hair, chuckling nervously. “I’m thinking of taking her to the Eiffel Tower.”

“Aw, really?” As usual, Evan was the first to bust balls. “Come on, man. That’s been done a million times.”

“Not for Ivy,” I reminded him. “It’s one of the

places she really wants to go, and she's never been. Why not give her the whole fantasy come to life?"

"We can't all propose while our girlfriend is in the middle of pushing out a baby," Miles pointed out with a smirk, referring to Evan's proposal. "That was peak romance."

"I think it sounds great," Noah told me, clapping me on the back. "And she'll love it."

"Yeah, congratulations." There was still a shadow that passed over Miles' face, which took a little of the sincerity out of his friendly smile. I was more interested than ever in whatever it was he had to tell me.

"This is between us," I reminded the guys as we continued up to the terrace, where the girls waited with an enormous lunch set up and waiting.

"There you are! We thought somebody got hurt on the way up here." Ivy practically skipped my way, wearing a light sundress that floated around her legs. "You smell like sunshine," she declared, touching her nose to my chest and inhaling deeply.

I lowered my head, murmuring in her ear, "How did it go?" From what I could see, everybody looked like they were in a decent mood. There were no tears, and the energy seemed positive overall.

"Pretty well," she said. "There were a few gowns

they really liked. It's just a matter of how much tailoring can be done by Saturday."

I knew the twins. They were still disappointed, though they tried to play it off. "It's not quite the same," I heard Aria tell Miles, and he rubbed her shoulders. "But it's gorgeous. I might even have chosen it if I had seen it before the dress I picked out. Maybe this is how it was supposed to be."

Ivy softly clicked her tongue as we approached the big table filled with so much food that I was surprised it didn't buckle under the weight. "They're really trying," she whispered, and I noticed the look she and Sienna exchanged. It was obvious they had worked together to keep things positive.

Rose had her own reasons to be upset. She exited the house with her phone in hand, and the way she frowned told me she hadn't gotten good news. "The fire chief says it might take a little more time to figure out the cause," she told Colton, raising her voice so the rest of us could hear.

"I hate to think it had something to do with the wiring," Colton mused, wrapping his arms around her when she leaned against him. "Who knows? An animal could've gotten in there, like a mouse or a squirrel, and started chewing. It happens."

"There's never been any history of shoddy work

in the family's business," Sienna pointed out. She was trying, and the grateful look Colton gave her said he noticed and appreciated it.

Rose gasped, shaking her head hard. "I would never blame you," she insisted, looking up at Colton. "I know all of those guys did the best work possible. That's never crossed my mind, I swear."

"You're going to be beautiful brides either way," Spencer assured the girls. "Nobody will be able to take their eyes off you."

"I don't know about anybody else, but I'm starving." Sienna grabbed a plate and began loading it with salad and grilled chicken. "You all had better hurry up if you want any of this."

"You're starting to sound like me," Valentina joked. Evan threw an arm around her, and she chuckled. It had to be a good sign, the fact that she could make a joke.

"How was the fishing?" Ivy asked, changing the subject as we got in line behind Sienna.

We managed to carry the conversation pretty well after that, and before long, the girls were laughing at the story of Colton's big catch turning out to be a discarded boot.

And while most of my attention was with them, a small part of me kept looking at Miles, waiting for him to give me a hint of when he wanted to talk. "You okay?" Ivy whispered at one point, touching her leg to mine under the table.

"Keep touching me like that, and I'll get pretty fucking uncomfortable," I murmured and grinned at the way her fair cheeks went pink.

"You look upset, is all."

"If I'm upset, it's because I didn't get a single bite on my line all morning." She seemed to accept that, going back to her lunch and making plans to visit the salon the following afternoon. Aria was going to dye her amethyst locks back to their natural brown for the wedding, something the girls assured her would look great and make her mom happy.

The staff started clearing our plates, which was when Miles looked my way and ever so slightly tipped his head toward the inside of the house. "Someone will need to direct me to the powder room," he announced as he stood. "I'm not very familiar with this palace."

"I'll show you," I quickly offered, and Ivy gave me a funny look that made me think I'd spoken too loudly. She didn't say anything, though, settling for watching us as we crossed the terrace and entered through French doors leading into the kitchen.

As soon as we were inside, away from the others,

he let out a sharp breath. "I need your word on something," he muttered as we crossed the kitchen, steering clear of the staff cleaning up after our feast.

"Sure. What is it?"

"Do not breathe the word of this. I don't want anything getting in the way of the wedding."

"Then you might want to brush up on your acting skills," I offered. "It's obvious there's something wrong."

"I've done my best to play it off," he insisted, looking over his shoulder as he went on. "But it seems like shit's getting worse all the time. I won't be able to keep this quiet for much longer. I only hope nothing comes out until after the wedding."

"Comes out?" There was nothing like finding out my suspicions were true when that was the last thing I wanted. Right away, images of a distraught Aria filled my head. Were we wrong to trust him after all the lies he had told in the beginning?

As soon as we were past the kitchen and in an empty hallway, I took him by his collar and pushed him against the wall. His eyes flew open wide before he shoved me away. "What the fuck?" he demanded.

I grabbed hold of him again and held him in place this time. "What did you do? I swear to God if you hurt her—"

"Enough, already." He held his hands up like he was surrendering. With his large frame and the skill he'd exhibited with his fists in the past, he could've easily taken me if he felt like it, but he gave up instead. "I didn't do anything to Aria, and I never would. This doesn't have to do with her directly, but I'm afraid it will affect her. I know it will."

I released him, backing up a step and folding my arms. "Talk. What is it you're hiding?"

A soft, familiar voice floated our way. "You know something?" Ivy asked as she rounded the doorway from the kitchen. Her arms were folded like mine, her jaw jutting out the way it sometimes did when she was irritated. "I would like to know that too."

Fuck. "Poison, we were—"

"Spare me." She sighed, her level gaze never leaving Miles. "I might not have been around when you originally came on the scene, but I know all about it, and I know how much that girl loves you. By the way..." she added with a roll of her eyes, "... you really suck at trying to be discreet. You both do," she finished, giving me a withering look.

"It doesn't matter," Miles said with a sigh of defeat that reflected in his troubled green eyes. "If anything, you might be able to help. Right now, I need all the help I can get."

6

LUCIAN

Ivy's arms were still folded, her now steely eyes narrowed, and I was almost knocked sideways at how insanely hot she was. That no-nonsense, take-no-shit-from-anybody attitude was one of the things that had made me fall for her in the first place.

Miles dropped into a leather armchair while Ivy perched gracefully on the corner of Ari's enormous desk as I closed the doors to Ari's study, leaving the three of us in relative seclusion.

"Tell us," I encouraged Miles, sitting in the chair facing him. He was miserable, slouching, one elbow propped on the chair's arm so he could hold his head up on his palm. "What happened? What do you need?"

"As you know, Spencer and I have been working together to patent a new device," he explained. I couldn't help but notice how defeated he sounded now. There was relief there, too, like he was glad he could drop the act and admit there was a problem.

He sighed, raking his fingers through his blond hair, letting his hand drop. "We have a competitor in California, someone Spencer used to work with years ago when he first got into the tech field. Damian Fields. He's a real piece of shit, the sort of guy who throws money at a team already on the verge of making a breakthrough, then claims that breakthrough as his own."

"That's a pretty common class of person," Ivy pointed out.

"He's also the kind of wanker who would stab a competitor in the back if it meant getting the jump on a patent, which is exactly what he's doing now," Miles continued with a snarl. "The son of a bitch has dug through my life, looking for something he can use to discredit me. And I'm afraid he's found it."

Now Ivy shifted slightly. She was uncomfortable, like me, and probably wished she hadn't demanded an explanation.

"What is it?" I pressed.

"I'm not proud of a lot of what I did in my

youth." He let out a bitter laugh while his lip curled in a sneer. "That's putting it mildly. I couldn't have imagined where I would end up, let's put it that way. I would have done a lot of things differently."

Right away, my mind went back to the first night he'd hung out with us when we watched him beat the shit out of a guy for getting aggressive with Aria. He didn't throw a punch like an amateur. I hadn't given it much thought until now when I wondered how much fighting a guy had to do to become that efficiently brutal.

He looked Ivy's way, frowning. "Like I said, I'm not proud. Aria knows about most of it, but not everything. I would appreciate it if you kept this from her, only sharing it when the time is right. I plan to tell her after the wedding."

Ivy's mouth fell open. "Hang on. That's not fair. If this is the kind of thing you don't want to tell her until after you're married, maybe she deserves to know now."

"Poison..." I whispered with a sinking heart. She had a point, sadly, though her blunt delivery lacked tact.

It hit him hard, making his features pinch together like he was in pain. "She's already dealing with the fire. All I want is for her to have the day she's always dreamed of. She doesn't need this."

"What *is* this?" I asked. "What is it she doesn't need?"

"It's bound to come out soon in the media. Which is why I wanted to talk to you," he explained. I watched as he tried to pull himself together, sitting up straight and pushing his hair back from his forehead. "I'm not asking for a cover-up, mind you. But I know damn well what he's going to put out there. His twisted version of the truth."

After he took a deep breath, he said, "When I was sixteen, I was in a pub in London. Back then, I was always looking for another reason to fight. I was pissed off all the time, wanting to take it out on somebody. I didn't like the way one of the lads was looking at me. He was posh, and I was anything but. I was raised to hate people like him." He slid an almost guilty look my way, one I instantly understood. He was raised to hate people like me.

He cleared his throat, then continued, "When he made the mistake of looking at me again, I charged at him and got in his face. Asked him what his fucking problem was. He threw the first punch." He made a point of telling us, looking back and forth like he wanted to be sure we believed him. "Not that I wouldn't have if he didn't beat me to it."

A lengthy pause followed. I was on the edge of my seat, and Ivy wasn't much better, her eyes glued to Miles while we waited. "The thing was..." he continued, "... he was practically blind drunk. The force of his swing made him lose his balance. He smashed his head against the edge of the bar when he fell."

"Jesus," Ivy whispered, covering her mouth with a trembling hand.

"I already had a record by then," Miles continued. "Fighting, minor vandalism. And I did start things according to the witnesses who spoke to the police. There was never any full agreement on whether or not I threw the first punch, but everyone agreed none of it would've happened if it weren't for me charging him the way I did. I paid a lot of money for legal counsel to have my record expunged, but money can also be used to hire investigators."

"So this Damian guy dug up the story?" I asked, wincing when Miles nodded.

"What happened to him?" Ivy asked in a tight voice. "The guy who fell."

Miles stared down at the hands now resting in his lap. "He suffered a traumatic brain injury. He was studying medicine," he explained in a heavy voice. "He's never walked again. He's only regained the ability to speak a few words. He needs constant care around the clock."

"Fuck, man." I sighed. What was there to say? "So Damian is going to use this against you to get the edge? Do you know when he plans on getting started?"

It could've been a trick of the light streaming through the window, but he looked a little green. "For all I know, the ball is already in motion. The story as he plans to tell it, of course, is about how I was a young punk who destroyed the brilliant future of a smart, ambitious young man who is now little better than a vegetable. It'll cause a scandal, naturally. My financial backers will vanish. He'll swoop in and claim the patent and make a mint. At least, that's what we're assuming."

"And I guess that's what Spencer was on the phone about this morning?" I asked. "The two of you looked pretty pissed off when he came down."

"He has people with their ears to the ground, watching and listening. His team out in Silicon Valley is working their asses off to pull everything together for the patent, but they're afraid it won't be fast enough, and then there's the possibility this asshole already got to one of the team members and is paying for info. He has the money to offer just about anything," he concluded, his anger and accent clipped the words until they were sharp as knives.

"He sounds like a real supervillain." Ivy winced as soon as the words were out of her mouth. "Sorry."

Miles only chuckled as he nodded slowly. "You're not wrong. The worst part is…" he shifted in the chair, uncomfortable, "… the contact Spencer spoke to earlier this morning reported at least one of Damian's associates was spotted in the Hamptons recently. Some thug on the payroll. Naturally, we're concerned he's been watching."

"Watching for what?" I asked.

"That's the thing. We don't know. We only know there's no reason for him to be out here unless it's to gain further leverage against me." He sounded sick and with plenty of reason to. I couldn't imagine having something like this hanging over my head two days before my wedding, worrying my fiancée would find out.

I looked toward Ivy, who now wore an expression I easily recognized. "You're already coming up with a plan, aren't you?" I asked.

"What do you think? Of course, I am." She chewed her lip, tapping her nails against the edge of the desk she sat on. "Sympathy. We're going to drum up sympathy."

"How?" Miles asked, exchanging a glance with me.

"There have been articles posted online about the fire at the store." Her brow wrinkled in concentration, eyes narrowed, and I had to wonder if she had any idea how absolutely captivating she was.

There was nothing as hot as the sight of her using her incredible brain. All I could do was sit back and let her work her magic.

She pushed away from the desk, pacing in tight circles in front of it. "We share those articles across all of our social media accounts," she suggested, talking more to herself than us. "We make sure to tag Miles or at least mention his name along with the others. This wedding has already gotten a ton of press coverage. We can play up this little plot twist as a tragedy but an opportunity for love to triumph. The wedding party keeping a stiff upper lip and all that. How nothing can get in the way of true love... I mean, look at this young man who clawed his way to the top despite the odds being against him. If a poor boy from London can find true love with a Manhattan princess, anything is possible."

"We'll beat them to the punch," Miles summed up. "I like it. I like the way you think."

"It's sort of my job to understand what people respond to," she pointed out with a small smile. "I want us to do everything we can to help things go smoothly."

"And I'll have team members set up Google alerts on your name," I assured him. "Their entire purpose for the next few days is to watch for anything having to do with you being shared online. We'll do everything in our power to drown Damian's shit out with all this goodwill we're drumming up."

He released a long breath, almost deflating like a balloon. "You have no idea what it means to hear you say that. Thank you both so much. I won't pretend you're doing this for me. I know it's for Aria and Valentina and everyone else. Making sure things are set for the wedding. But I'm still grateful."

"Let Spencer know we're on it," I told him, standing, shaking his hand, and patting his shoulder. "And for fuck's sake, try to compartmentalize a little better."

Ivy nodded sagely, her ponytail swinging. "You have a terrible poker face."

"I'll keep that in mind," he replied with a smirk. "I always thought I did, but I've never been in a position like this. Thank you. Thank you for keeping this between us. I promise you, Aria will know soon enough about this. Not yet, though. She doesn't need one more thing weighing on her mind."

I noticed the way Ivy stayed quiet, the way her frown deepened. Silence spread between us for a few moments after Miles went out to join the group.

Finally, she groaned, spreading her arms in a helpless shrug. "I don't feel good about this. I'm sorry, but I don't."

"You don't believe him?"

I was glad when she shook her head. "It's not that. I'm sure he was telling the truth, and the whole thing was an accident. I know how cutthroat business can get too. It's Aria I'm worried about. She deserves to know about this."

"And she will."

"Right. Not until after the wedding. It feels... well, it feels icky," she concluded. "Like we're tricking her somehow."

"I don't think it's that serious. But if you don't feel right about it, I'll handle things." Wrapping my arms around her, I added, "All we're doing is making sure nothing else goes wrong this weekend. Aria doesn't need to know about this right now. It would only be one more thing to get in the way of celebrating."

"Just like a man." There was a lot of love in the way she said it, but more than a little exasperation too. "You think you're protecting us at times like this. You might know Aria better than I do, but I'm a woman like she is. I'd resent having the truth kept from me like I'm being patronized."

When she put it that way, I understood. "Let her and Miles work it out for themselves," I decided, kissing her forehead. "We have to trust them."

"Fine. I will," she said. "I hope if all of this is true and that guy did send some thug out here, they aren't going to cause trouble."

"Let's try not to worry about it," I urged, staring out the window over the top of her head. That was easier said than done now that my imagination was running away with me.

Was I being paranoid... or did it seem like too big of a coincidence for the store to burn down when it did?

7

EVAN

"This place is going to be fantastic." Colton lined up his shot, eyeing the flag on the seventh hole. He was in no hurry, considering we had the entire course to ourselves the day before the wedding. "It's the perfect addition to your properties."

"And just think," Lucian pointed out as we watched Colton putt. "At the very least, our dads will keep the place in business."

Colton sank his putt, laughing. "I'm starting to think the entire reason for having the estate out here is so Dad can golf whenever he wants."

"Can you blame him?" I asked as I gazed around at my latest purchase. My tenth property. The sale had closed a few months shy of my thirtieth birthday. The way I had always planned my life.

It didn't feel real, but then not much about the last six months did. The last two years as a matter of fact. I'd never imagined Valentina being the woman I needed to complete my life—to give it meaning. None of my success would have been worth a damn if I didn't have her and Isabel at the end of the day. There had been a time when I would've laughed at a sentiment like that. What an arrogant dumbass I used to be.

"I have to admit, I'm impressed." It was Spencer's turn, though he seemed more interested in admiring the surroundings than in putting. I couldn't pretend there was no pride involved as I watched him look around, nodding in approval. "You say you're planning on expanding?"

"No, I was referring to my property in Greenwich," I explained, exchanging a grin with Colton. "He gave me the idea a couple of years ago before his wedding. I purchased a large plot of land that borders my country club and golf course, and the groundbreaking for the resort will take place in a couple of weeks."

Spencer smirked. "Let me guess. The family company is managing construction."

"How was I going to pass up that opportunity?" Colton asked with a laugh.

"Have you ever considered going bicoastal?" Spencer asked when he'd sunk his putt. "God knows there are plenty of properties like this in my area... golf courses, country clubs, resorts. A good friend of mine out there is looking to free up some liquid assets, in fact, and he has a handful of properties he's looking to unload. I could connect the two of you."

"I think his brain just exploded," Lucian observed, chuckling. "You should have waited until after the wedding to ask a question like that. I hope he can pull it together by tomorrow afternoon."

"Fuck off," I muttered, getting a laugh from everybody else. "If there's one thing I'm going to get right, it's my vows. Certain things a guy doesn't fuck up."

"Are you boys sure you don't want me to take you out tonight?" Spencer looked around the group, eyeing Miles and me in particular. "It doesn't have to get crazy. I'll have you back before curfew."

Miles and I exchanged a glance. I couldn't speak for him, but I knew what my answer was. It took no thought. "Funny, but I'm really not interested. Not that I want to hold anybody else back," I added. "You can go get your drink on. I'll be fine with whatever is served at the rehearsal dinner."

"We've changed," Noah announced. "All I want at the end of the day is to be with Sienna. If I have to go out of town, I want her to come with me. Normally, she can't since she has her own shit going on. But I miss the hell out of her during those trips."

"Back in the day, that would have meant a fresh crop of women to work your way through," I pointed out, thinking back on those days. It hadn't been all that long ago—only a few years.

But it was long enough to change everything. Two of us were fathers, and all of us were either married, engaged, or about to be.

"You know what's funny?" Lucian asked, lining up his putt. "Back in the day, when we were kids, our dads used to say the same thing. About how they were domesticated. Remember?"

"You mean the 'hunkholes?' " Colton asked, making air quotes with his fingers. "All the stories about their glory days, fucking their way through Manhattan?"

Noah groaned. "Shit. Are you saying we've turned into our fathers?" He looked around, then glanced down at his polo shirt and khakis. "Shit. We're starting to dress like them."

"Personally, I hope not," I pointed out, since my father was not somebody I was looking to emulate. Our relationship would never be more than tentative. We held each other at arm's length, mostly because he didn't know how to live any other way.

Thinking of him turned my thoughts to Isabel. I didn't know much about being a good father, but I knew the father I didn't want to be. My daughter would never wonder how I felt about her. She would never ask herself if my work mattered more than she did. She would never see anything other than love and respect between her mother and me. That much was for damn sure. We would give her the same sort of loving, stable example Magnus and Evelyn had given Valentina.

All of that was on my mind long after we finished our game and drove back to the estate. Tonight, the guys and I would stay at Ari and Olivia's house while the girls remained with Barrett and Lourde. They wanted to keep the whole tradition alive of the groom not seeing the bride in advance.

I wanted to make sure I had everything I needed packed up in preparation. More than that, I wanted to spend a little time with my family. The rush of last-minute fittings meant I didn't have a lot of time with Valentina. She was stressed and distracted, and I hoped as I climbed the stairs that she would be able to enjoy herself a little bit tonight. But by the time we finished rehearsing and sat down to dinner, her worries about what she was wearing tomorrow would ideally be nonexistent. It would be a shame if, after all this anticipation, she couldn't at least take a second to take in the moment.

The door to our guest room sat partly open, meaning I could hear what was going on inside. Soft giggles drifted out into the hall, making me tread quietly, creeping up to the door so I wouldn't disturb anything.

There they were—my reason for living. Isabel was on the bed, looking freshly changed while Valentina tickled her feet. "Stinky piggies!" she squealed, holding one of Isabel's chubby little ankles in one hand, touching her nose to the sole of her foot. "Pew! Stinky piggies!" Isabel dissolved in giggles, making Valentina laugh again.

She had always been beautiful. I would never forget the first day I set eyes on her and how she blew me away. Her personality, dry sense of humor, and sarcasm had solidified that. Everything about her had clicked for me from the beginning.

Now that she was a mother, I had the pleasure of getting to know this other side of someone I thought I knew so well—her sweetness, softness, endless patience. She was living, breathing love, and she had helped me find a side of myself I didn't know existed.

A floorboard creaked beneath my feet and her head snapped up, her smile widening when she found me watching. "Look who it is," she whispered to Isabel, whose face lit up when she saw me.

She clapped her chubby hands. "Daddy! Daddy, look!" I knew what I had to do when she held up a bare foot.

I owned ten properties and was on the verge of building a sprawling resort. Hundreds of people depended on me to make good decisions that would keep them employed. Yet when my little girl wanted me to sniff her foot, what was I supposed to do but inhale and collapse on the floor? When she squealed, it was all worth it. I would've done it all day long if it meant hearing that sound.

"I was just about to put this one down for her nap." Valentina was still laughing as she stood and picked up Isabel, setting her on her hip. They shared the same clear, blue eyes that now danced with happiness. "Then I was thinking of taking a nap, myself. I don't think I can make it through the rehearsal if I don't."

I followed her into the small room that connected our guest room with the one Colton and Rose had chosen. A pair of cribs were set up in there, and Valentina laid Isabel in hers before turning on a white noise machine. "Eloise will be here soon," she whispered, stroking the baby's curls. "You get a good nap."

I took her hand and led her back to our room, closing the door softly while murmuring, "I'll never get tired of seeing the two of you together. You know that?"

"I always feel the same way whenever you two are playing, or you're rocking her to sleep." She turned to me, wrapping her arms around my waist and kissing me softly, whispering, "I fell in love with you a long time ago, but seeing you as a dad has made me love you in a whole different way. Does that sound silly?"

"Are you kidding? Nothing could sound better." I kissed her, deeper this time, cradling her head in my hands, my fingers sinking into her thick, brown waves. The most precious thing, and she loved me. She was going to marry me. My wife. The thought made me rock-hard in an instant.

"I hope you're not too tired," I managed between kisses as I backed her up against the bed. "Though this doesn't have to take long..."

She blurted out a laugh, sat down, and reached for my belt. Watching her built my anticipation, promising good things to come as she unbuttoned my khakis. "Please. You know I'm no match for your powers of seduction, especially when you talk dirty like that."

I took her chin in my hand, tipping her head back to stare into her blue eyes. Eyes I could have drowned in. "How about I tell you I can't wait for our honeymoon so I can worship every inch of your body for two solid weeks?"

Her nostrils flared as she sighed, then lowered my zipper. "That's an improvement."

I closed my eyes at the first lap of her tongue against my hard, swollen cock. Sheer pleasure sizzled through me the way it always did. All I needed was her touch. "Do that again," I grunted out, then groaned my approval when she did—just one thing of so many that set her apart.

She took pride in giving great head because she enjoyed it. She got off on every sound I made and the way my breath quickened.

"That's right, suck my cock," I whispered while

she did just that—rolled her tongue around my ridge and plunged down again. "Take all of me. Let me feel you swallow around my head." I hissed in a breath as her throat contracted, my thighs tensing with the sudden burst of pleasure that shot up my spine. "Fuck... is your pussy dripping for me? For my cock? I want to sink so deep inside you. Is that what you want?"

She moaned her response, increasing the pressure until it was almost too much. I was already coming close to the edge. "You want me to fuck you, don't you?" I asked, bucking my hips in time with her hot mouth.

Releasing me, she panted while stroking me with her tight fist. "Seems like you won't last long," she taunted, a wicked smile played over her swollen lips. "Why don't you check and see how wet I am?" My heart almost stopped when she hiked up her dress, spreading her thighs.

What else could I do but accept the invitation? I leaned over her, pushing her back against the mattress. Hovering over her, I brushed my mouth against hers while I delved between her legs with my fingers. The crotch of her panties was wet, and my cock jumped at the first touch.

To hell with taking it slow. I could barely wait for

her panties to be tossed aside before I impaled her, standing next to the bed with her ass on the edge, her legs against my chest. She was too good, too tempting. Her pussy was too sweet and much too wet to be denied for even as long as it took to get undressed.

"Shi-it... that's it," she whimpered as she moved with me. "I love it when you fuck me. I love *you*..."

"And I love you. This pussy..." Spreading her legs, I stripped off my shirt, then leaned down to hold her closer. She wrapped her legs around my hips and pulled me deeper while I ran my mouth over her jaw, down her throat, savoring her sweet sighs. I could imagine loving her this way for the rest of my life, and I looked forward to it.

"Come with me," she whispered, breathing faster now, her nails scraping my skin as she ran them over my back. I didn't have a choice. I was close enough before I entered her, and now all it took was her muffled moan as she bit her lip and her pussy clenching with her release for me to let go.

"Do me a favor." I pushed myself up on my forearms to look down at her flushed, shining face. "If marriage changes us, promise me it'll never change that."

"Oh, trust me," she whispered with a grin. "I'll want you until the day I die, Evan Anderson. You'll have to beg me to lay off you."

There weren't many things I knew for sure, but I knew that was an impossibility.

8

EVAN

"Do you remember that one Christmas in Vail when you invited me to come along with you guys?" I settled into one of the chairs on the back terrace of the Goldsmith estate, a scotch in hand.

The night was quiet and still. The calm before the storm, maybe. This time tomorrow, I'd be a married man.

Colton chuckled, nodding. "That's right. We had a great time, didn't we?"

"Easy for you to say," Noah snorted from his chair, stretching his legs out and propping his feet on the edge of the table. "You're not the one who spent half the time with a broken arm."

"Hey. Nobody told you to drink in the hot tub,"

Lucian reminded him. "Whose dumbass fault is it that you slipped and fell getting out?"

"I thought your mom was going to kill you," I told him, raising the pitch of my voice and wagging a finger. "I turn my back on you for one minute, and now you're going to spend Christmas Day with your arm in a cast."

"Watch it with the impersonation," Noah warned, chuckling. "She's somewhere inside, and she has superhuman hearing."

"You couldn't use the new skis your parents bought you, either." Colton snickered, adding, "You're lucky I was nice enough to break them in for you."

Noah pointed at him from across the table, his face going red in the glow of lights strung overhead. "I knew that was you! And you spent the next week telling me it wasn't!"

"It wasn't my fault you were so doped up on painkillers that you were out of it when we left for the slopes." Colton ducked out of the way of the crumpled-up napkin Noah threw at him, making us all laugh.

Miles shook his head, swirling scotch in his glass. "I don't know if I've ever said this out loud, but the four of you are damn lucky to have what you have. This shared history."

"You're part of it now," I reminded him. "And we have years ahead of us."

"Yeah, you're marrying into the madness," Lucian joked. "There's no escaping. Sorry about that."

"No need to apologize. I couldn't be happier." Miles had a funny way of showing it since he looked miserable as hell, even when he tried to play it off the way he did now by offering a humorless chuckle. "I only hope Aria is never sorry she decided to get mixed up with me." Was it my imagination, or did he and Lucian exchange a look?

I glanced at Colton, but he was oblivious, reading something on his phone. "Rose says the girls are having a sleepover party the way they used to back in the day. I guess we're all thinking along the same lines tonight."

"It's a shame we're here and not there," Noah mused as he poured another drink from the vintage Macallan bottle sitting in the center of the table. Ari had broken it out for us when we arrived after the rehearsal dinner, a special gift on a special night. It was buttery, smooth like velvet as it rolled down my throat and spread warmth through my chest.

"Yeah, we could play pranks on them the way we

used to," I laughed. It had been years since I thought about it. "When was it that we fucked with them when they were playing with that Ouija board? At the cabin in New Hampshire? I think we were all still in high school."

"I've never heard about this," Miles reminded us. "What did you do?"

"Nothing major." Colton's lips twitched like he tried to hold back laughter. "We just went out to the breaker box and fucked with the lights to make the girls think they had made contact with a ghost. No big deal."

"Remember the way they screamed?" Noah's head fell back as he let out a hearty laugh. "We could hear them from outside with all the doors and windows shut. They really thought they were opening a portal to another dimension or some shit."

"Right," Lucian recalled. "And when they told our parents when they got home from being out, we all got our asses chewed."

I waved a hand. "I could tell your dads were trying not to laugh, even when they were telling us off. The kind of thing a parent has to do at a time like that."

"You know that's going to be us someday, right?"

Colton pointed out. "They'll think we're hypocrites, the way I always thought my dad was a hypocrite. It hasn't been too long since I felt that way, come to think of it."

We fell into silence, all of us lost in our thoughts. It took an event like this to get a man thinking about the past, the future, and the choices he made. I would never regret mine. Hell, it was torture being without Valentina for a single night. I couldn't remember the last night I hadn't checked in on Isabel at least once, just to be sure she was all right.

"I would like to make a toast." Colton tapped the table with his palm, picking up the bottle of scotch. "Come on. Glasses."

"What are we drinking to?" I asked.

"The hell do you think?" he asked, rolling his eyes. "I swear. They'll have to engrave 'It was just a joke' on your headstone someday. We're drinking to us. Somehow, we managed to find the women we will never deserve but who, for some reason, put up with us."

"So we're drinking to them never running out of patience with us?" Miles asked.

"Something like that." When we were all ready, Colton raised his glass. "To the future. Whatever it holds, we'll be able to get through it together."

"I think I can drink to that," Noah announced, tapping his glass to Colton's. We all did the same, toasting each other before draining our glasses.

However, as we did it again, I couldn't help noticing Miles' hesitation. The way his smile slipped.

WHY THE HELL was I so jittery?

"I can't believe I'm nervous. This is insane." I had to laugh at myself as I drummed my knees with my hands while the limo pulled out of the Goldsmith driveway and turned onto the street, taking me that much closer to my future. There wasn't a doubt in my mind that I'd found the perfect woman—the other half of my soul.

We had gotten a beautiful day, and I hoped as I stared out the window that Valentina could relax a little now that we knew the weather wouldn't be a problem today. There were so many little things that could go wrong, though granted, neither of us had anticipated losing the entire bridal party's outfits so close to the big day.

"It's not insane," Colton assured me. "If it is, that means I'm insane too. I was nervous as hell."

"It only means you're human," Lucian insisted. "There's nothing to be nervous about. Nobody pays attention to the groom, anyway."

"Thanks for your support." I snickered while pulling out my phone. I had been texting Valentina throughout the morning, and the last message was to tell her we were getting ready to leave. Sure, a lot of it had to do with making sure she felt all right today. Part of it, though, was my need to reach out to her.

This was a day that had been years in the making. Whenever I thought about it that way, a profound sense of gratitude washed over me. That, and the need to connect with her in any way I could.

Me: *I can't wait to see you. How is Isabel? Behaving, I hope?*

Valentina: *She's an angel. Wait until you see her. You'll die, she's so cute.*

Me: *I hope I don't since that would mean not getting to see you.*

"The photographers are here," Colton observed as we pulled into the front courtyard of the Black estate. "Shit. Whoever was in charge of decorating must have worked through the night."

When I looked up from my phone, I saw what he meant. It didn't seem possible for the exterior of the house to be so elaborately decorated in a matter of hours, but the results were in front of me by the time we came to a stop. One of the hired staff opened the limo door, and I stepped out, ignoring the clicking of shutters all around me as the photographers documented this moment. Candid shots were better, anyway, meaning we would always be able to look back on my open-mouthed surprise.

The porch railing was draped in lush floral garland with lanterns hanging from the eaves and vines of flowers wound around the columns. There were more lanterns on posts staked into the ground running along the edge of the driveway and courtyard with the same floral garland draped between them. The scent of the flowers was almost overwhelming, but in a good way, stirred by the breeze coming off the water.

"This is incredible," Miles announced with a smile as he took it in. "I honestly didn't expect it to be this... beautiful."

"Wait until you see what they've set up in back." Evelyn stepped out onto the porch wearing a floor-length, pale pink dress that sparkled a little when she moved. "You won't be able to believe your eyes."

"You look lovely," I told her, kissing her cheek once she reached us. "How are the girls holding up?"

"Like I said. You won't be able to believe your eyes." She winked, accepting Miles' kiss. "I can't believe it. I'm gaining two sons today. Everything is changing so fast."

"For the better?" I asked, making her laugh gently.

"You know it's for the better, smarty." We paused for photos, then walked around the perimeter of the house instead of through and possibly seeing something we weren't supposed to just yet.

"Have my parents arrived?" I asked, scanning the random clusters of people already scattered across the back lawn. Evelyn wasn't kidding. The set-up for the ceremony was beyond what I had imagined. Rows of chairs were divided by a white runner wide enough for Magnus to walk both Aria and Valentina at the same time. On both sides of the runner, at the beginning of every row, there was a lush arrangement of roses, lilies, hydrangeas, and flowers I didn't recognize. Along the outside of the rows, thick pillars had been set in place.

If today had turned out rainy, a tent would have been set up over them, but there was no need for that. Instead, more of the same garland was swagged between them and ran overhead until there was practically a ceiling of flowers. Every so often, a petal or two would drift down when the breeze blew.

At the end of the runner was the elaborate archway set up over the raised platform where a string quartet warmed up. Photographers wandered in and out, taking candid shots, while the officiant chatted with Magnus and Barrett. However, I couldn't find my parents anywhere.

"I'm sure they'll be here soon," Evelyn offered. "It's a shame they couldn't spend the weekend with us."

"I'm pretty sure they were both afraid the other one would show up," I joked. "Believe me. Having them under the same roof would have made the weekend miserable."

"Did you eat today?" she asked, going into Mom mode. It was probably easier to fall back on habit than to reflect on her daughters getting married in less than an hour. "I can't have either of you passing out in the middle of the ceremony."

"And risk getting this dirty?" Miles asked, brushing a hand down the front of his navy suit. "Aria would have my head."

"You can wear a bib if you need to," she retorted, laughing. "There's a ton of food inside. I'll fix you both a little plate and tie a napkin around your neck."

Miles smiled fondly as he watched her retreat into the house. The roar of activity inside was audible as soon as she opened the door. "I've wondered so many times what my life would have been if I'd been raised by a mother like her," he admitted.

It was rare for him to open up like that. We all knew his mother had been no picnic, putting it mildly. She had made it her life's mission to twist him up inside, feeding him lies and blaming Magnus and Evelyn for all of her problems back when Miles was a baby. He had gone through a lot of shit to make it to where he was today, sitting on top of a tech empire, about to marry into a large, loving family like the Millers and everyone who came with them.

"To tell you the truth, I've wondered the same thing for years." Gazing over the grounds again, my heart sank a little. "My parents can't be bothered to show up early enough for us to have a few minutes before the ceremony. I wouldn't be surprised if they were both waiting for the other one to arrive first so they wouldn't have to bump into each other out in the courtyard."

"I'm sure they'll pull it together for your sake today," he offered, though, of course, that was the sort of thing a person said at a time like this.

"Still," I mused. "Everything turned out the way it was supposed to. Right? If anything in our lives went slightly differently, we wouldn't be here now."

"You sound downright philosophical. Are you sure you're feeling well?" He touched the back of his hand on my forehead, and I shoved his arm away, both of us laughing.

We were roughly twenty minutes from the start of the ceremony by the time Dad arrived, shortly followed by my mother and her boyfriend, Scotty. It would've been nice if she had left him at home, considering it seemed the only reason she brought him was to show off in front of Dad.

"Do you think I could get a photo with just the two of you?" I asked her as she hung on Scotty's arm like they'd accidentally glued themselves together.

"I'm sure you haven't forgotten how to stand on your own two legs," Dad muttered, scowling at her as he adjusted his cuffs and tie. "Unless you're feeling a little unsteady in your old age."

This was everything Valentina and I would never be. I couldn't imagine ever speaking to her like that or disrespecting her in any way, especially in front of Isabel, no matter how old she was.

I was more sure of myself than ever by the time Colton offered to show them to their seats. "Rose texted," he murmured, escorting Mom. I noticed she didn't mind letting go of Scotty if it meant taking his arm instead. "They're almost ready to go in there."

This was it.

My pulse picked up speed, but there were no more nerves. Now, it was all about anticipation. My head was on a swivel, searching for Miles. I had lost sight of him while dealing with my parents. I caught Noah's eye and mouthed the word Miles, but he only shrugged.

I walked around the house's perimeter, greeting a few guests in passing, one eye trained for him. Finally, I found him on the front porch, pacing while staring at the floor and rubbing the back of his neck with one hand. The other he shook out like he was nervous, and now I noticed how rapidly he was breathing. *Cold feet?* He would have to be the stupidest bastard in history if he was rethinking marrying Aria.

"Hey. We're just about ready back there." I didn't want to overwhelm him, considering he looked like he was in pain, but this couldn't be avoided. "Are you feeling all right? Do you need another minute?"

"I don't think so." He came to a stop, then heaved a sigh. "I don't think another minute is going to help."

"What are you saying?" I asked, dreading the answer.

"I'm saying I don't think I can go through with this."

9
——————
MILES

It was out there. I couldn't take it back. And now that I'd said it, I knew it was true. What had been festering in me for days had been voiced.

Unfortunately, that meant giving Evan a mild heart attack from the looks of it. "What?" He jogged up the front steps, facing me with his mouth hanging open and his eyes bulging. "No. You don't mean that."

"I know what I mean. I can't do it to her."

"To her?" He had to whisper the way I did. There was no telling who might be inside and possibly able to hear. "She's marrying you today because she wants to. What are you talking about, doing anything to her? You know Aria. She only does what she wants to."

He didn't get it, but then how could he? "You're misunderstanding me," I explained. "It isn't that I don't want to marry her. I can't go through with it without her knowing about something I've kept from her. I told myself it could wait until after the wedding, but now I know I was wrong."

"Okay. We can work with that." He looked like somebody had his balls in a vice, no matter how supportive he tried to sound.

I knew the feeling too well since my balls had ached painfully in the weeks since Damian had made it known he intended to pursue a patent for the same technology Spencer and I were working to develop. Every day, the pressure had ratcheted up a little more. Now, it was a miracle I could walk.

He checked his watch, looking toward the cars parked in front of the house, managed by a valet. Thinking about the guests, I guessed. "What can we do?" he asked. "Do you need to talk to her?"

Fuck. All of the worries I had fought to suppress bubbled up to the surface with that one loaded question. *Did I want to talk to her?*

It was the only way. Ever since that conversation

with Lucian and Ivy, there had been a hole growing in me, like an ulcer, but much larger and more painful. Guilt would do that to a person.

I hadn't known this depth of guilt in two years. Not since I discovered everything I'd ever believed about Magnus and Evelyn had been a lie. That they weren't the monsters my mother had portrayed them as. There were times when that terrible night came back to me in dreams—nightmares, really. The horror of realizing what I had done, the instant certainty that Aria would never forgive me for lying, seducing her, and working against her family. There had never been a more helpless, horrified moment in my life. Not even when I knew there was nothing I could do to keep my mother alive.

Now, I had to wonder if I could keep my relationship alive. What was worse, telling her now about what I had done or waiting for her heart to break when I eventually came clean?

I'd spent the last several days with my heart in my throat, always waiting for something terrible to happen. Something Damian put in motion. Obsessively checking to see if there was any mention of me online. Waiting for Aria's normally loving, gentle smile to turn into something born of horror and disgust.

I should've told her sooner. Damn me for being a coward. For being afraid of losing her, of losing the one good thing that had ever come out of my otherwise pointless life. None of it meant anything without her.

I couldn't look into that shining face of hers and recite my vows while knowing there was something so pivotal she was unaware of. "I'm not sure how we can do it." I sighed, shrugging. "But yes, I should talk to her."

He gave me a firm nod. "I'll see what I can do."

Five minutes later, I stepped into Barrett's study, leaving the door open a few inches and standing behind it. Suddenly, we were in the middle of a sitcom, a bride and groom conversing from either side of a door so there wouldn't be any accidental eye contact.

As strange and awkward as it was, there was something reassuring about it too. I might be able to get the story out easier and faster if it meant not having to watch pain and disbelief take root. I didn't want to watch disappointment dim the light in her eyes.

"Here she is," Colton announced, hidden by the door. "We'll be waiting outside." His footsteps faded away as a familiar hand snaked its way around the door, feeling for mine.

"You in there?" Aria's soft laughter may as well have been a knife to my heart. She was nervous, of course, and confused.

"I'm here." I took her hand, lacing our fingers together, clasping it tight.

"What's happening? Why are we doing this? Please, don't tell me you're having second thoughts." Another soft laugh, this time tight with dread.

I hated knowing that was where her mind immediately went. "Not about you, love," I told her, squeezing her hand. "Never about you. If you don't believe anything else, believe that."

"I appreciate it, but I hope you understand you're not doing anything to make me feel better." Her laughter was flat now like she didn't have it in her to pretend. "What gives? We've got hundreds of people waiting out there, not to mention another couple who are waiting on us."

My mouth went dry. I couldn't find the words. What was I supposed to say? How to approach this delicately?

She must have taken my silence for something else because when she spoke again, her voice was ominously quiet. "Miles," she whispered. "Tell me.

Whatever it is, we'll get through it. Just tell me and get it over with before I die of nervousness."

"It's about the patent... well, not really," I amended. Already, I was fucking up. "There's something out there about me. It will be public soon, and the person who spreads it is going to spin it to turn me into a villain and put my leadership in question. It's all a matter of stealing the technology out from under us and claiming the patent for himself."

"You couldn't tell me about this before?" she asked. "I'm still lost."

"It's all about what's going to come out in the press." This was it. This was when I found out whether or not she truly meant it when she said we could get through anything. Not that I would blame her if she walked away. Certain things were insurmountable.

"Tell me. Don't you trust me?" she whispered.

"With all of me. It's just that... I want to make sure you trust me with you, and I'm afraid you won't anymore. You see... there was an accident years ago. A bar fight, or it would've been if the other guy had managed to land a punch. He fell. It resulted in a traumatic brain injury. I was locked up in a juvenile facility for a year because of it. My record was cleared once I had the resources to get it done."

"Oh." That was all she said. It was more of a heavy breath than a word.

Now that I had started, I couldn't stop. "I was charged because I lunged at him, but I never touched him. He was drunk. He lost his balance. He could've died," I admitted. "But he didn't. And as soon as I started making money, I took his care in my hands. I've paid for every cent of it since. The best money can buy."

"But whoever spreads this story isn't going to mention that part. Only that you supposedly almost killed somebody?"

"That's it. I've been waiting for it," I confessed. "Spencer has been running interference. He knows this guy, or at least knows of him. He's seen what he's capable of. Frankly, I'm stunned the story didn't come out this weekend to coincide with the wedding."

When too many heartbeats passed without a response, I gripped her hand tighter. "Please, I need you to understand. I wasn't trying to hide this as much as I was keeping it to myself out of shame. I would've told you eventually. It's the one thing I'm most ashamed of."

"You said you didn't touch him."

"And I didn't. I never had the chance. But if I

hadn't tried to start shit with him because of the chip on my shoulder, we wouldn't be having this conversation. He was everything I wasn't, wrapped up in a single person. Posh, surrounded by friends, confident, well-dressed. He symbolized everything I had missed out on. You know the way my mind worked back then."

"I know," she murmured, her thumb stroking mine. That one tiny gesture gave me hope. She wouldn't touch me that way if she didn't love me.

"He would be living a normal life now if I hadn't decided to provoke him. No amount of money can make up for what he lost because of my stupidity."

"You've done everything you could to make it right. And I know you're sorry for it because I know your heart. I wouldn't marry you if you were some heartless, cruel person. I love you."

"Still?"

"Miles, nothing is going to change that. So get that out of your head here and now. I'm not going anywhere except down that aisle the way we planned."

"You know, things could get messy in the press."

"I don't care about that beyond your stress. I know the truth. I know who you are."

"You thought you knew who I was before I told you this. Maybe you don't know me all that well."

"I know why you did what you did. For all the reasons you described. I know what you went through. So no, it doesn't surprise me to hear you tried to pick a fight with some rich kid in a bar when you were a teenager."

Her voice softened, and her grip on my hand tightened as she continued, "It also doesn't surprise me that you would pour money into his care. No, you can't undo the past, but you've done everything you could to make it right. That's exactly the kind of man I know you are. So I'm not surprised, and I'm not changing my mind about going through with this wedding if that's what you're most worried about."

"I won't pretend it's not a concern," I admitted.

"You have nothing to worry about. We're getting married today," she insisted. "And I'm going to be by your side no matter what happens. Got it?"

My chest was about to burst. I should've told her from the beginning. When would I learn to trust her? "I love you." The words didn't begin to cover the depth of my feelings. My gratitude.

"You'd damn well better because everybody's out there waiting for us." She gave my hand one more squeeze, giggling. "Now, I'm going to go hide by the back door while you go out through the front. Okay?"

"Okay." Before she could run away, I pressed my lips to the back of her hand. "Thank you."

"Don't thank me. Just get your ass outside." Then she was gone, leaving me smiling in relief. A massive weight had left my shoulders. It was enough to make me wonder how I had functioned before now, weighed down the way I was. There would still be trouble in the press—I wasn't naïve enough to think Lucian and Ivy could clean everything up all at once —but I had Aria's love.

I wasted no time getting outside and rounding the house. Evan visibly relaxed when he spotted me from where he stood in front of the platform. When I reached him, he whispered, "Do me a favor and don't ever fuck with me like that again. I kid you not when I say my life flashed before my eyes."

"It won't happen again," I promised. Before I could express my apologies, the quartet began to play, and two hundred people turned in their seats to watch the girls walk down the aisle.

First came the matter of the flower girls. It sounded like Evan was having trouble breathing when Isabel began toddling our way, one hand wrapped around the handle of a small basket while Eloise held the other side. They wore matching dresses, white with full skirts, and both tossed rose petals in virtually all directions while guests chuckled and took videos.

"Daddy!' Isabel was only a few feet away when she abandoned the basket and came running, arms outstretched, her soft brown curls bouncing. Evan bent down to hug her when Evelyn lured her away to sit with Lourde and Barrett.

The bridesmaids came next, wearing dresses in a shade of dusty rose. I had heard Aria mention the color more times than I could count while we were going over the wedding plans. Ivy was first, followed by Rose. Sienna was Maid of Honor, and I couldn't help but notice the meaningful looks that she and Noah exchanged as she drew closer. They were probably imagining themselves as the bride and groom someday soon.

The music shifted, signaling the guests to stand for the brides. This was it. I couldn't have imagined loving Aria more, but she had proven me wrong by hearing the most shameful memory of my life and loving me anyway. Now, I was about to marry her.

Guests gasped when the twins came into view with Magnus between them. I couldn't draw enough air into my lungs to gasp. Aria literally took my breath away in a lace dress that hugged her body from the strapless neckline to the short train behind it. For the sake of a more classic look—her words—she had dyed her hair to a shade close to its natural brown. It was pulled back, showing off the dangling diamond earrings I'd bought her as a wedding gift. They didn't sparkle half the way her smile did, even underneath a veil.

Valentina had gone with a different look, in a full-skirted dress sewn with pearls and crystals that sparkled whenever she moved. "Oh my God," Evan whispered, sounding like somebody had kicked him in the stomach. I understood the feeling. My entire future was coming toward me, looking like an angel.

I stepped up to the platform's edge a few feet from where Evan waited. Magnus came to a stop with the girls in front of us, turning to them and exchanging a few words, then taking a step backward. For a second, his face contorted like he was fighting back tears, but he managed to make it through while we led the girls up onto the platform and stopped in front of the officiant.

"You are exquisite," I whispered to Aria after she'd handed her bouquet to Rose. "You look like a dream."

Taking my hands in hers, her blue eyes sparkling with tears, she replied, "I think I'm the one who's dreaming."

"A happy dream, I hope?"

Her radiant smile floored me. "The happiest I ever had."

10

MILES

"I can't believe how beautiful it all is." My bride gaped at the decorations under the tent where we would soon eat dinner. The tent beside it was designated for dancing, and both were as crammed with flowers and flickering lanterns as the rest of the grounds. "It's magical."

Valentina bounced Isabel on her hip, pointing out the flowers, admiring how the candlelight made the crystal on every table sparkle. "Isn't it pretty, sweetie?"

"I have to admit." Evan gave a nod of approval. "I'm sorry I was such a pain in the ass when it came to making decisions about this stuff. I thought it didn't really matter much either way. Now I see I was wrong."

"Hold on, everybody." Valentina staggered slightly, fanning herself. "Stop the presses. Evan Anderson admitted he was wrong about something."

"This is what I get for being sincere." He shrugged at me. "I'm glad you're here to witness this. I did try."

We had spent the better part of cocktail hour having photos taken, and soon, guests would start wandering in here. I was glad to have a few minutes to ourselves, so I could watch Aria's joy play out across her face, to see the candlelight reflected in her eyes. Time was ticking, however.

"I have to go up and get changed into my reception dress," she announced.

That was news to me. "Reception dress?" Now that I took a closer look at Valentina, it occurred to me she had already changed into a simpler but no less stunning version of the dress she'd worn during the ceremony. "Since when?"

"Since there was no way I was going to be able to sit down and eat a bite in this." Aria ran her hands down her sides, laughing. "Those seamstresses took their job seriously. I don't even know if I could take a sip of water."

"Hurry up and get changed," Valentina urged. "We have to make our big entrance together."

"Why do I feel like we are only accessories in all of this?" I asked Evan, who was still laughing as Aria pulled me from inside the tent. We were like a couple of delinquents sneaking out of school, rushing up to the house before anyone could catch us and demand a few minutes of our time.

"I can't believe the ceremony is over," she admitted as soon as we were in the kitchen, ducking our way past rushing servers running around with trays. It was a relief to make it to the hall, which was considerably less hectic.

"It passed by in a blink, didn't it?" I asked on our way to the foyer.

"It doesn't seem fair for something that took all this planning to pass so quickly." She picked up her train and started up the stairs. "I want to stop time. I want to hold onto this as long as I can."

I understood what she meant. I wished I could capture her this way, to freeze her in place in this moment of joy. "All you can do is enjoy it," I reasoned as we reached our room, where I locked the door behind us just in case anyone decided to come looking.

A much simpler white dress hung on the back of the closet door. Aria took it from the hanger and draped it over the back of an armchair while carefully removing her veil and setting it down. She then turned her back on me. "Help me with this? There's, like, a hundred buttons."

"My first task as a husband. I'm honored." We laughed as I began my way down the seemingly endless row of satin-covered buttons. "Holy hell. How long did it take to get this buttoned up?"

"It felt like an eternity."

I touched my lips to her back, noticing the way she shivered. "You have never been so radiant," I whispered, slowly easing the dress away from her body, kissing the skin I exposed until the heavy lace-covered satin puddled around her ankles, and she was in nothing but a white strapless bra and a thong. Hunger announced itself deep in my core and started to unfurl, spreading to my dick and thickening it at once.

She turned slowly, took my face between her hands, and planted a slow, lingering kiss against my mouth. "You know what I just realized?" she whispered, trailing her fingers down my cheek. "Our marriage isn't official yet."

And this was why we were meant for each other since I was thinking along similar lines. "That's a good point," I murmured, pretending to be a lot more solemn than I felt while my dick hardened.

"I mean, reciting vows is one thing." As she spoke, she slid my jacket from my shoulders, then neatly laid it across the foot of the bed, turning back to me. This time, she worked on my belt. "And signing a marriage license is all fine and good, but until you consummate the marriage, it's all for nothing. It's kind of dumb, but it is true."

"It would be a shame if lightning struck me down, and we couldn't make this official," I pointed out, watching her fight back a grin.

"Wouldn't it?" The button slipped free, then she unzipped my fly, backing me up against the bed and sitting me down, my slacks and boxer briefs around my knees. "We really should do something about that."

My arms slid around her so I could unhook her bra, and her gorgeous tits tumbled free. I wasted no time taking them in my hands, caressing them until her eyelids fluttered. "What did you have in mind?" I asked, taking one of them into my mouth, sucking her nipple so it hardened, watching her succumb to pleasure.

"I have a few ideas," she whispered, moaning when I used my tongue to flick the tip of her tight nipple. "Why don't you lie down, and I'll show you?" She nudged me back, and I obliged, propped on my elbows so I could watch as she lowered her thong.

I would never get tired of this. Watching light play over her smooth, firm body as she straddled me. The thrill of her touch when she took me in her hand and guided me inside her incredibly tight pussy. Her soft, open-mouth gasp when I first stretched her and the sigh that followed as she lowered herself to my base.

"Congratulations," she said, grinning down at me. "We're officially married."

"Are you sure about that?" I took her hips in my hands. "Because I'm fairly sure we both need to finish for it to be official."

She dropped onto her palms, one on either side of me, her grin widening. "I guess we shouldn't leave anything to chance," she whispered as her hips began to move.

"By all means." I loved nothing more than watching her like this—claiming her pleasure and using me to get her there. Her soft grunts left me almost frantic to consume all of her.

My wife.

Finally, my wife.

She leaned down, breathing hard, and I caught her juicy bottom lip between my teeth, giving a playful nip. "Careful," she warned between gasps while my hands slid down her smooth back. "Don't mark the bride on her big day."

"Can't have that, can we?" Instead, I settled for digging my fingers into her firm ass until she whined, grinding on my cock. "I'll just have to mark you where nobody else can see."

Her eyes closed as a deep sigh parted her lips. My God, there wasn't anything more stunning in the world than her like this, lost in a passion that built with every sensual stroke, every grind of her hips.

My senses were overloaded. Yet it was profound gratitude that ruled over every other thought. I'd never been so grateful for her—a woman who knew me, all of me, yet was determined to love me anyway with her enormous heart and her luscious body.

A body that now moved faster while we kissed, panting into each other's mouths, working together toward the end. "Come with me," she urged when a moan stirred, the sort that left my balls aching and ready for release. Then the tightening of her pussy, the increased friction, pushed me toward the edge of a cliff I'd fallen over with her many times.

"Yes, love," I whispered, holding her hips and jerking her onto me to meet my thrusts as I drove into her. "Jesus, you're squeezing me so fucking tight... I'm not going to be able to hold back much longer. Come for me, *now,*" I gritted out, my breath catching.

"Oh, yes... yes, Miles... I'm..." She ended with a gasp, her head snapping back in the instant before her pussy began to milk my shaft. The pleasure of letting go was nothing to the pleasure of watching bliss turn her already precious, perfect face into something no artist could capture.

Ethereal, exquisite.

And mine. Always.

"I GUESS it's time for me to make my speech." Colton stood, microphone in hand, while the staff cleared our dinner plates. "First off, I would like to speak for my parents when I thank all of you for joining us here at our family estate. It's been a privilege holding an event like this, but especially for people who mean as much to us as these four."

He looked at Valentina, then at Aria, and his smile softened. "I'm so glad we grew up the way we did, as close as we did. It's even better that we're still close all these years later. I hope we never lose that since you two are part of the fabric of my life.

Evan..." he continued, "... you've been a brother to me. I can't imagine anyone making Valentina as happy as you do, and I know for a fact that you need her to keep you in line, but there's nobody better for that job."

Knowing laughter rang out in the tent.

"Miles..." he concluded when the laughter died down, "... you have been a welcome addition to our group and our family. You fit in seamlessly, and I'm sure that couldn't have been easy with all the history between us. I know Aria was worth the effort."

I smiled at my wife, covering her hand with mine. She had been more than worth the effort, which didn't feel like effort at all. I was a lucky man in so many ways.

"Please, everyone." Colton lifted his champagne flute, signaling for the guests to do the same. I noticed Evelyn dabbing her eyes with a napkin, and for the second time today, it looked like Magnus was fighting back tears as he gazed at his daughters. "To the happy couples. May the rest of their lives be filled with as much love and joy as they feel today."

The twins got up to hug their cousin once his toast was finished while the emcee for the evening announced dancing was about to kick off in the adjoining tent. "Come on!" Aria rushed over to me, grabbed my hand, and pulled me out of my chair. "You owe me at least one dance."

"Already with the demands when we've barely been married four hours." I kissed her hand, then let her go. "I'll be there in a minute. Go ahead, shake your ass. I'll meet you there."

"Don't keep me waiting," she warned, heading off with Sienna and Ivy.

Lucian trailed behind them, but I flagged him down before I could lose sight of him, pulling him aside to murmur, "I wanted to thank you for keeping everything under wraps for me. Ivy was right. I should've told Aria from the beginning. Now she knows, and we're ready to face whatever comes next."

"We're right here, ready to help you," he assured me. "But for tonight, try to forget about it. Don't let this guy ruin a once-in-a-lifetime night."

"You're right. He doesn't deserve the power." I must have been convincing since he settled for shaking my hand without offering more advice. "Now you'd better snag Ivy before some lazy, arrogant playboy tries to pick her up."

His head snapped back. "She would never fall for a guy like that," he scoffed, and we laughed as he followed the crowd into the next tent. I wasn't in a hurry, and not because I wanted to hang around while the servers set up the dessert stations.

Spencer was at the bar, ordering a drink while eyeing a pair of cute blondes. "I thought you were flying out tomorrow afternoon," I said when I reached him, nodding toward the girls who pretended not to notice his attention.

"Yes, not for another... eighteen hours," he confirmed, checking his watch. "I can get a hell of a lot done in eighteen hours."

"We aren't flying out to Maui till Wednesday," I reminded him. "Keep me posted on everything when you get home and meet with the team."

He drew a deep breath, taking a sip of his drink. "I didn't know whether to bring this up tonight or later, but I was talking with Connor and Barrett during cocktail hour." He turned his head slowly to one side, then the other, casually checking for any eavesdroppers before continuing. "Barrett received a call from the fire chief. They're calling it arson."

My heart sank like lead. "Based on what evidence?"

"Traces of accelerant detected on several surfaces." Our eyes met as he added, "The same accelerant used in two suspicious fires in the Bay area within the past year."

I didn't want to believe it, but this was how Damian Fields operated. He would stop at nothing to get what he wanted, and at the end of the day, the lengths he was willing to go to make a smear campaign look like child's play. "Let me guess. Damian's competitors?"

He nodded slowly. "I have to admit, I've wondered since Wednesday night if he was behind it. Knowing about the other fires, knowing how he loves sending a message, it all makes sense. I didn't want to say anything until we had proof."

"One hell of a message," I growled out, observing the party while seeing none of it. Instead, I saw the burning timber and the smoke that rose from it. I heard the heartbroken sobs of Aria and her sister, and the memory twisted my guts. "He wants to burn us both down no matter if it means hurting the people around us."

"Especially if it means that," Spencer corrected. "Message received."

"What's next?" I asked. "You know him better than I do. What do we do now?"

His slow, knowing smile hinted at a man much more ruthless than the image he presented to his family. "Now, we get to decide the sort of message we want to send back."

I was slightly shaken by the time the sounds of music and laughter drew me to the adjoining tent, where strings of lights twinkled beneath the canvas overhead, and dozens of people crammed onto the floor. The brides danced in the center of the large group, holding each other's hands and belting out the lyrics to a pop song.

Tonight was about them. About us. I wasn't about to let Damian Fields destroy another moment. We would handle him when the time came.

"Excuse me," I called out after almost fighting my way through the crowd once the song ended. "I'm going to steal her from you," I told Valentina, who blew me a kiss, launching into another dance when the next song began.

"Isn't it great?" Aria's flushed face shone, her baby blues sparkling. "I love you so much!"

"I love you," I told her, then laughed when she shimmied to an even faster, pounding tune. I'd never seen her glow so radiantly or be so carefree.

Holding out her hands, she called out, "Dance with me!"

There was only one thing for a groom to do in a situation like that. Nobody would ever call me a dancer, but for my bride's happiness, I would do my level best... tonight and always.

WANT MORE BILLIONAIRE PLAYBOYS?

Introducing....

The Elite Men of Los Angeles

Coming 2025

ALSO BY MISSY WALKER

ELITE HEIRS OF MANHATTAN SERIES

Seductive Hearts

Sweet Surrender

Sinful Desires

Silent Cravings

Sensual Games

Endless Love

ELITE MEN OF MANHATTAN SERIES

Forbidden Lust*

Forbidden Love*

Lost Love

Missing Love

Guarded Love

Infinite Love Novella

A White Christmas with the Blacks

ELITE MAFIA OF NEW YORK SERIES

Cruel Lust*

Stolen Love

Finding Love

Hungry Heart

Chained Heart

Iron Heart

Trusting the Rockstar

Trusting the Ex

Trusting the Player

*Forbidden Lust/Love are a duet and to be read in order.

*Cruel Lust is a trilogy and to be read in order

All other books are stand alones.

JOIN MISSY'S BOOK BABES

Hear about exclusive book releases, teasers, discounts and book bundles before anyone else.

Sign up to Missy's newsletter here: www.authormissywalker.com

Become part of Missy's Facebook Reader Group where we chat all things books, releases and of course fun giveaways!

https://www.facebook.com/groups/ missywalkersbookbabes

ACKNOWLEDGMENTS

Thank you so much for reading about the Heirs! Your love for the Elite Men inspired me to continue this series and explore where they are now. I truly hope you enjoyed this journey. While it's hard to top the Elite Men, writing about all these characters has been a joy, and I've loved every moment of bringing their stories to life.

Massive thanks to my rockstar editors—Chantell, Kay, and Nicki—you ladies saved me! And to my beta squad—Ella, Karmin, Maria, and Saskia—you've been beyond patient and I owe you big!

To my awesome fans, especially my Facebook crew, Missy Walker's Book Babes—this community is everything, and your love and support keeps me going!

Much love,
Missy x

ABOUT THE AUTHOR

Missy is an Australian author who writes kissing books with equal parts angst and steam. Stories about billionaires, forbidden romance, and second chances roll around in her mind probably more than they ought to.

When she's not writing, she's taking care of her two daughters and doting husband and conjuring up her next saucy plot.

Inspired by the acreage she lives on, Missy regularly distracts herself by visiting her orchard, baking naughty but delicious foods, and socialising with her girl squad.

Then there's her overweight cat—Charlie, chickens, and border collie dog—Benji if she needed another excuse to pass the time.

If you like Missy Walker's books, consider leaving a review and following her here:

instagram.com/missywalkerauthor
facebook.com/AuthorMissyWalker
tiktok.com/@authormissywalker
bookbub.com/profile/missy-walker

9 781923 036222